Emethystin

Privilege of Death

JAYA MAYA JAISWAL

BLUEROSE PUBLISHERS
India | U.K.

Copyright © Jaya MayaJaiswal 2025

All rights reserved by author. No part of this publication may be reproduced, stored in a retrieval system or transmitted in any form or by any means, electronic, mechanical, photocopying, recording or otherwise, without the prior permission of the author. Although every precaution has been taken to verify the accuracy of the information contained herein, the publisher assumes no responsibility for any errors or omissions. No liability is assumed for damages that may result from the use of information contained within.

BlueRose Publishers takes no responsibility for any damages, losses, or liabilities that may arise from the use or misuse of the information, products, or services provided in this publication.

For permissions requests or inquiries regarding this publication, please contact:

BLUEROSE PUBLISHERS
www.BlueRoseONE.com
info@bluerosepublishers.com
+91 8882 898 898
+4407342408967

ISBN: 978-93-7018-433-6

First Edition: March 2025

Disclaimer

This story is a work of fiction. Any resemblance to actual persons, living or dead, or real events is purely coincidental. The characters, settings, and incidents are products of the author's imagination and are not based on real-life occurrences.

Chapter : 1	The Marked Healer of Thistledown
Chapter : 2	Whispers of the Forbidden Grove
Chapter : 3	The Journey to the Kingdom
Chapter : 4	The Kingdom's Threshold
Chapter : 5	The Prince and The Secret
Chapter : 6	Secrets in the Moonlight
Chapter : 7	The Dim Light Castle
Chapter : 8	The Other Half of the Scripture and Lost Lyra
Chapter : 9	The Mysterious Althea
Chapter : 10	Market Encounters & Friendship
Chapter : 11	The Strike of Allies and Revelations
Chapter : 12	A Friend's Warning
Chapter : 13	The Storm Within & Silent Wounds

Chapter : 14	Healing and the Haunting Truth
Chapter : 15	Forging the Path & Echoes of Strategy
Chapter : 16	The Sword of Destiny & The Shadow of Death
Chapter : 17	The Crossroads of Change
Chapter : 18	Whispers of a New Dawn & The Oracle's Truth
Chapter : 19	The Knife Behind the Smile
Chapter : 20	The Captive and The Crooked King
Chapter : 21	A Rescue or Escape?
Chapter : 22	The Scars We Carry.
Chapter : 23	A Fractured Sanctuary
Chapter : 24	The Workshop Reunion
Chapter : 25	The Festival and the Spell
Chapter : 26	The Ugly Creature & The Spirit World

Chapter : 27	Silent Struggles & The Confession
Chapter : 28	The Bonfire Revelation
Chapter : 29	The Return of the Lost
Chapter : 30	The Gathering Storm
Chapter : 31	The Final Hunt of the Pink Moon
Chapter : 32	When Death Called Her Name

Chapter 1

The Marked Healer

of

Thistledown

The forest whispered secrets to those who dared to listen. **Emethystin** had always been one of those listeners. At nineteen, she moved through the dense woods with the grace of a deer, every step deliberate and silent. The western forest village of **Thistledown** had been her home since birth, a place where the trees loomed large and ancient, their roots intertwining with the lives of the villagers.

Emethy's life had never been ordinary. She was born with a peculiar mark on her back, just below her left shoulder—a swirling pattern, almost like a crescent moon entwined with intricate vines. The village elders spoke in hushed tones about the mark, calling it the Sigil of the Healer. It was said to be a gift, a rare blessing bestowed upon those chosen by the forest itself.

Her gift had manifested early. At the age of five, she had healed a wounded rabbit she found near the edge of the village. By the time she was ten, the villagers had come to rely on her for the well-being of their livestock and the creatures of the forest. She had an uncanny ability to understand their pain, soothe their fears, and mend their wounds with her touch.

This morning, as the first light of dawn filtered through the canopy, Emethy made her way to the glade where she often found solace. The air was cool and fresh, filled with the scent of pine and earth. She carried a small leather pouch filled with herbs and poultices, ready for any creature that might need her help.

As she reached the glade, she noticed something unusual. The birds were silent, and a heavy stillness hung in the air. Her heart quickened, and she felt a twinge of unease. She stepped cautiously into the clearing, her eyes scanning for any sign of distress.

Emethy's gaze followed the unique bird, its feathers shimmering with hues she had never seen before.

Mesmerized, she stepped deeper into the forest, her curiosity pulling her forward. The bird darted gracefully between the glowing trees, and she quickened her pace, eager to see where it would lead. Suddenly, she noticed the fading light around her and the growing shadows of dusk. Panic prickled her skin as she realized it was almost nightfall. Her aunt would be furious if she returned late again. Reluctantly, she turned back, casting one last glance at the mysterious bird as it disappeared into the forest depths.

When she finally reached the outskirts of Thistledown, she could see the small cottage she shared with her aunt. Smoke curled lazily from the chimney, a sign that breakfast was likely being prepared. Emethystin quickened her pace, but the moment she stepped inside, she was met with her aunt's stern gaze.

"Where have you been, child?" her aunt demanded, her voice edged with frustration. Aunt Marella was a woman of few words and many expectations, and Emethy had long since learned that her aunt's scoldings came from a place of deep care, though they stung all the same.

"I was in the glade," Emethy replied, lowering her eyes. "There was a wounded deer—I had to help it."

Marella's expression softened for a moment, but only just. "You know better than to wander off so early. This forest is no place for a young woman to be roaming alone, especially one with your... abilities."

Emethy winced at the mention of her gift. "I'm sorry, Aunt Marella. I just couldn't miss it."

Her aunt sighed, placing a hand on Emethy's shoulder. "I know you mean well, but you must be careful. Your gift is powerful, but it also draws attention—attention we may not want."

Emethy nodded, understanding the unspoken warning. The villagers may have accepted her abilities, but there were others who might see her as a threat, or worse, as a tool to be used. The weight of her gift had always been a burden she bore quietly, but moments like this made her acutely aware of the dangers that came with it.

"Come, sit down and eat something," Marella said, her tone softening further. "And promise me you'll be more cautious in the future."

"I promise," Emethy replied, giving her aunt a small, grateful smile.

As they sat down to the simple meal, the tension between them eased, and the warmth of the hearth seemed to chase away the lingering chill of the forest. But as Emethy ate, her thoughts remained with the deer in the glade, and the strange stillness that had settled over the woods that morning. Something was changing, and deep down, she knew her life was about to take a path as winding and unpredictable as the forest itself.

The moon hung low and full, casting an eerie glow over the village of Thistledown. Emethystin stood at the edge of the forest, her heart pounding in her chest. The mark on her back, a twisted vine-like pattern just below her right shoulder, tingled with an unsettling warmth. She knew what was coming, and she hated it.

Ever since she was a child, the birthmark had been a source of both wonder and fear. On nights like this, when the full moon illuminated the world in a ghostly light, the mark would glow with a soft, pulsing radiance. She had learned to hide it, wrapping herself in thick cloaks or staying indoors until the night passed. But tonight, something felt different.

Emethy pulled her cloak tighter around her, her eyes scanning the darkened trees. The forest seemed to be holding its breath, as if it knew her secret and was waiting for her next move. She could hear the whispers of the trees, their leaves rustling with unspoken words. The wind carried faint voices, murmurs that only she could understand.

"Emethy," the wind seemed to sigh, "come closer."

She took a deep breath, steeling herself. She was no stranger to the voices of the forest; they had been her companions for as long as she could remember. The river's gentle rumblings, the crackling of fire, the whispering breeze—they all spoke to her, guiding her, comforting her. But tonight, their voices held an edge of urgency.

With a determined stride, Emethy ventured deeper into the woods. Her heart raced, but her steps were sure. She had always been daring, never one to shy away from the unknown. It was this fearlessness that had made her the village's healer, the one people turned to when their animals were sick or injured. Her connection to the forest and its creatures was unparalleled, and she wore her role with pride.

As she walked, the glow from her mark intensified, casting a faint light through her cloak. She winced, wishing she could will it away. The villagers would never understand—they might even fear her if they knew. The mark was a reminder of her difference, a beacon that set her apart.

"Emethy," the river's voice rumbled, louder now. "You must hurry."

She quickened her pace, her breath coming in short, sharp bursts. The path ahead opened into a small clearing, the moonlight flooding the space with an ethereal glow. In the centre of the clearing lay a wounded fox, its fur matted with blood. Emethy's heart ached at the sight.

Kneeling beside the fox, she gently touched its side. "Shh, it's alright," she whispered. The warmth from her mark spread through her hand, and she felt the familiar surge of energy. The fox's breathing steadied, its eyes blinking open to gaze at her with gratitude.

As she worked, a sudden gust of wind whipped through the clearing, carrying with it a voice that was both familiar and foreign. "Emethy," it whispered, "your destiny awaits."

She looked up, her eyes narrowing. "Who's there?" she demanded, her voice edged with defiance.

From the shadows stepped a figure cloaked in darkness, their face hidden. "Do not be afraid," the figure said, their voice a soft, melodic hum. "I am here to help you."

Emethy's hand moved to the dagger at her waist. "Why should I trust you?"

The figure paused, then slowly lowered their hood to reveal a face both stern and kind. "Because we share a common enemy," they said, echoing the words she had heard so many times in her dreams. "And because you are unique from the others. "

Emethy's mind raced. The forest had always been her ally, her confidant. But to be told she was chosen, destined for something greater—it was almost too much to bear.

"Why me?" she asked, her voice trembling slightly. "What makes me so special?"

The figure smiled gently. "Your mark," they said, "is a gift, a sign of your unique connection to the elements. The forest, the air, the fire, the rivers—they all speak to you because you are their guardian."

Emethy swallowed hard, the weight of the words settling over her. She had always known she was different, but this revelation was overwhelming. "What must I do?" she asked, her voice barely more than a whisper.

The figure extended a hand. "Join me," they said. "Together, we can protect this land from the darkness that threatens it."

Emethy hesitated, her thoughts a whirlwind of fear and uncertainty. But as she glanced back at the fox, now resting peacefully, she knew she couldn't turn away.

Taking a deep breath, she reached out and clasped the stranger's hand. But Emethy declined the proposal since she preferred to be alone herself. And with that, Emethy's journey into the heart of her destiny began.

Her instincts warned her that the spirit was not to be trusted, its presence wrapped in an aura of unease she couldn't shake. Yet, she didn't know why spirits were drawn to her in the first place. It was as if something about her called to them—a mystery she couldn't unravel, no matter how hard she tried to ignore it.

Chapter 2

Whispers of the Forbidden Grove

Emethy had grown up with death as a constant companion. The shadow of loss had touched her life too many times, stealing away friends, neighbours, and loved ones. She remembered the faces of those she had lost—her childhood friend Lily, who had been like a sister, taken by a fever that even Emethy's healing touch could not abate; the kind old man from the neighbouring cottage who had tended to the village gardens; and the young mother who had passed away during childbirth, leaving behind a wailing infant. These memories haunted her, fuelling a deep-seated hatred for death and a fervent desire to save every life she could.

Despite her fearlessness and skill as a healer, there was one place in the forest she was forbidden to enter—the Grove of Lumina. The elders spoke of it in hushed tones, warning of its dangers and mysteries. The grove was said to be a place of unparalleled beauty, where fireflies glowed like embers and the leaves of the trees shimmered with an otherworldly light. Emethy had always been drawn to it, sensing a pull that she couldn't quite explain. The voices of the forest spoke of the grove with reverence, hinting at its secrets.

One evening, as the sun dipped below the horizon and the full moon began to rise, Emethy felt an inexplicable urge to venture towards the forbidden grove. She had just finished tending to the village animals and was about to return home when a strange feeling washed over her. It was as if the forest itself was calling her, guiding her steps.

Ignoring the warnings that echoed in her mind, she followed the pull, moving deeper into the forest. The path grew darker, the air thicker with anticipation. As she approached the grove, the familiar whispers of the trees grew louder, mingling with the murmurs of the wind and the gentle rumble of the nearby river.

"Emethy," the voices beckoned, "come to us."

The moment she crossed the threshold into the grove, she was enveloped in a soft, ethereal glow. The fireflies danced around her, their lights creating intricate patterns in the air. The leaves of the trees shimmered like precious gemstones, casting a luminescent light over the clearing. It was more breathtaking than she had ever imagined, and for a moment, she forgot her fears and the warnings of the elders.

But then, she saw him who she refused earlier.

At the centre of the grove lay an injured man, his body battered and bruised. Blood stained the ground beneath him, and his breathing was shallow and laboured. Emethy's heart lurched. Who was he, and how had he come to be here?

She approached cautiously, her healer's instincts taking over. "Can you hear me?" she asked, her voice gentle but urgent.

The man's eyes fluttered open, and he gazed at her with a mixture of pain and relief. "Help me," he whispered, his voice barely audible.

Emethy knelt beside him, quickly assessing his injuries. He had several deep cuts and a nasty gash on his side. She reached into her pouch for her herbs and poultices, her hands moving with practiced precision. As she worked, she couldn't shake the feeling that there was something strange about this man, something otherworldly.

"What happened to you?" she asked, trying to keep him conscious.

He winced in pain but managed to speak. "I was... attacked. Something in the forest... it's coming. You must leave."

Emethy's blood ran cold. "What's coming?" she demanded, but the man had already lost consciousness.

Fear gripped her, but she pushed it aside, focusing on stabilizing the man's condition. She applied her healing herbs and murmured a quiet incantation, channelling the warmth from her birthmark into his wounds. The glowing mark pulsed with light, and slowly, the man's breathing steadied.

Just as she was beginning to feel a glimmer of hope, a chilling sound echoed through the grove—a low, guttural growl that sent shivers down her spine. Emethy looked up, her eyes scanning the darkness. The trees whispered warnings, and the fireflies' light flickered nervously.

"Emethy," the wind sighed, "you must leave now."

She glanced at the man, torn between the need to save him and the urge to flee. But something inside her—perhaps the same force that had drawn her to the grove—compelled her to stay.

"I won't leave him," she said firmly, her voice steady despite the fear coursing through her veins. She stood protectively over the man, her dagger drawn and ready.

The growling grew louder, and shadows began to move at the edge of the grove. Emethy's heart pounded as she prepared to face whatever threat was coming. The grove, once a place of ethereal beauty, now felt ominous and foreboding.

As the first of the creatures emerged from the shadows, Emethy tightened her grip on her dagger. She didn't know what awaited her, but she knew she couldn't let fear control her. She was the forest's guardian, and she would protect it—and the man—at all costs.

And so, with her birthmark glowing brightly covered with cloak under the moon light and the voices of the elements guiding her, Emethy stood her ground, ready to face the darkness that threatened her home. The growling shadows dissipated as quickly as they had appeared, leaving the grove silent once more. Emethy's grip on her dagger loosened as a soft, ethereal glow emerged from the darkness. She blinked, trying to make sense of what she was seeing. Floating before her was a spirit, a young girl no older than twelve, her translucent form glowing with a gentle light.

Emethy's breath caught in her throat. The spirit looked at her with wide, innocent eyes, and she felt an overwhelming sense of love and sorrow emanating from the child.

"You're... a spirit," Emethy murmured, lowering her dagger.

The girl nodded, her form flickering slightly. "I am. My name is Lyra. You don't have to be afraid, Emethy."

"How do you know my name?" Emethy asked, her voice tinged with suspicion.

Lyra's expression softened. "The forest speaks of you. It knows your heart, your pain." She glanced at the unconscious man. "He has done terrible things. He is being punished by a dark spirit."

Emethy frowned. "Punished? For what?"

Lyra's gaze grew distant, as if she were trying to recall a foggy memory. "I don't remember everything, but I see the darkness that follows him. He hurt many people. The spirit that punishes him is powerful and full of anger."

Emethy felt a pang of sympathy for the child, but she hardened her resolve. "I can't let him die," she said firmly. "I don't care about his past. He's hurt and needs my help."

Lyra's eyes filled with sadness. "Be careful, Emethy. The darkness that follows him might come for you too."

Emethy ignored the warning and focused on the man. She lifted him gently, supporting his weight as she began the trek back to her village. Lyra followed silently, her presence a constant reminder of the supernatural forces at play.

When Emethy finally reached her home, she laid the man on a makeshift bed in the corner of her small cabin. Exhausted, she collapsed onto a stool, her mind racing with questions and doubts. Lyra hovered nearby, watching her with a mix of curiosity and concern.

The next evening, Emethy joined her aunt for their regular sword practice in the clearing behind their home. Her aunt, a formidable woman with years of battle experience, had taken it upon herself to teach Emethy the art of swordsmanship. It was their way of bonding and ensuring Emethy could protect herself in a world full of dangers.

As they sparred, Emethy noticed Lyra watching from behind a tree, her eyes wide with fascination. She tried to ignore the spirit, focusing instead on the movements of her blade and the rhythm of their practice. But Lyra's presence was a constant distraction.

"Emethy, you're not concentrating," her aunt chided, swinging her sword in a wide arc. Emethy barely managed to deflect the blow; her thoughts scattered.

"Sorry, Aunt Marella," she muttered, glancing briefly at the spirit.

Marella followed her gaze but saw nothing. "What are you looking at?"

"Nothing," Emethy lied, shaking her head. "Just tired."

After practice, Emethy retreated to her room, hoping for some solitude. But Lyra followed her, hovering at the edge of the room like a silent shadow. Emethy could feel the spirit's eyes on her, and it made her uneasy.

"Why are you still here?" Emethy finally asked, her voice sharper than she intended.

Lyra's expression was forlorn. "I have nowhere else to go. And I feel safe with you."

Emethy sighed, her resolve softening a little. "Just... don't get in the way."

Days turned into weeks, and Lyra became a constant presence in Emethy's life. The spirit asked endless questions about everything—about Emethy's childhood, her healing abilities, her fears and dreams. Emethy, though initially cold and distant, found herself answering in spite of herself. There was something disarming about Lyra's innocence, something that made

Emethy's heart ache with a long-buried longing for companionship.

One evening, while rummaging through her aunt's trunk for supplies, Emethy found an old, dusty scripture. The leather-bound book was worn and fragile, its pages filled with ancient runes and cryptic illustrations. As she carefully turned the pages, a sense of foreboding washed over her.

"What is it?" Lyra asked, peering over her shoulder.

Emethy's eyes narrowed as she studied the strange symbols. "I don't know. But I think it's important."

Lyra's form flickered with excitement. "Maybe it holds the answers you seek."

Emethy closed the book, a chill running down her spine. "Or maybe it brings more questions."

As she placed the scripture back in the trunk, she couldn't shake the feeling that she had just uncovered something that would change everything. The darkness that Lyra had spoken of, the man's mysterious past, and her own destiny—all seemed intertwined in ways she couldn't yet understand.

"And with that, the next chapter of her journey loomed ahead, shrouded in mystery and danger."

Emethy knew she needed help deciphering the ancient scripture, so she took the book to Old Eamon, the village's sage and the only person she knew who could read and write. Eamon's eyes widened as he examined the text, but after a few moments, he shook his head in frustration. "I can make out some of it," he said, his voice heavy with regret, "but it's in a dialect I don't fully understand. You need to find someone more knowledgeable." He paused, then added, "There's an old kingdom to the east, where a woman named Seraphina lives. She's a keeper of ancient lore and can likely interpret this for you." Determined, Emethy set her resolve, knowing her journey from the forest village to the distant kingdom was just beginning.

Emethy returned home and approached her aunt again. "Aunt Marella, I need to go to the old kingdom to find Seraphina. She can help decipher the scripture."

Marella's face darkened. "No, Emethy. You have responsibilities here. There is much work to be done in the village."

"But Aunt Marella, I feel this is important. I need to know what it says," Emethy pleaded.

"You are not to go. The village needs you," her aunt said sternly, her voice leaving no room for argument.

Emethy felt frustration welling up inside her. "I just want to see what it looks like. It might hold answers that could help us all."

Marella's eyes softened slightly, but her resolve remained firm. "The world outside is dangerous, Emethy. Stay here and fulfil your duties."

Reluctantly, Emethy nodded, knowing it was not the time to argue further. As she packed her things and prepared to leave the next morning, the words of the scripture echoed in her mind, a promise of answers and perhaps more questions.

With Lyra by her side, Emethy stepped into the forest, her path illuminated by the moon's silvery glow. The journey ahead was fraught with uncertainty, but Emethy felt a newfound sense of purpose. The spirit's tale had only just begun, and Emethy was ready to uncover the secrets that lay hidden in the shadows.

"In the heart of darkness, the light reveals the truth."

Chapter 3

The Journey to the Kingdom

Lyra & Emethy set out on their journey to the old kingdom, leaving behind the familiar safety of Elderglen and venturing into the unknown. The path ahead was filled with wonders that neither had ever imagined. They traversed lush meadows where flowers seemed to sing in the wind, crossed bridges over chasms that echoed with ancient whispers, and passed through forests where the trees themselves seemed to bow in greeting.

Lyra's eyes were wide with wonder at every turn. She giggled with delight at the sight of a family of deer frolicking in a sun-dappled glen and marvelled at the glowing mushrooms that lit their way through a darkened grove. Emethy, despite her usual stoic nature, found herself smiling at Lyra's innocent joy. The spirit's laughter was a welcome reprieve from the weight of her responsibilities and the dark memories that haunted her.

One evening, as they neared a crystal-clear river, Emethy decided to collect water for their journey. The river's surface shimmered like liquid silver under the moonlight, casting a serene glow over the surrounding landscape. Emethy knelt at the riverbank, her mind focused on the task at hand, when she sensed a sudden shift in the air.

From the shadows emerged a figure, its eyes glowing with an unnatural light. A demon, twisted and dark, stepped forward, blocking Emethy's path. Lyra, sensing the danger, hid behind a nearby tree, her form flickering with fear.

The demon's voice was a guttural snarl. "You do not belong here, girl. Turn back or face my wrath."

Emethy stood her ground, her hand instinctively moving to her dagger. "I have a destination to reach and no time to mingle with you," she replied, her voice steady and fearless. She had heard countless stories of demons since childhood and had always been prepared to face them.

The demon roared in anger, lunging towards her. Emethy met its attack with swift precision, her movements honed from years of sword practice with her aunt. The fight was fierce, and the demon's strength was formidable, but Emethy's resolve was unbreakable. As they clashed, the clouds parted, allowing the full moon's light to bathe the scene in a ghostly glow. Her birthmark, hidden beneath her cloak, began to shine with an intense light, illuminating the darkness around her.

The demon faltered, its eyes widening in fear as it beheld the glowing mark. With a sudden, reverent motion, it dropped to its knees before her, its earlier malice replaced by awe. Emethy, surprised but not letting her guard down, kept her weapon ready.

"What is this?" she demanded, her eyes fixed on the demon.

The demon's voice was a whisper now, filled with a strange reverence. "The mark of the chosen," it murmured. "Forgive me."

Emethy watched as the demon retreated into the shadows, its presence dissipating like mist in the morning sun. She took a deep breath, the tension in her muscles slowly easing. She turned and made her way back to where Lyra was hiding.

"The demon is gone," Emethy said, her voice gentle as she approached the frightened spirit.

Lyra emerged from her hiding place, her form flickering with relief. "I was so scared," she admitted. "I know that demon. It was after me."

Emethy frowned, puzzled. "Why didn't you tell me?"

Lyra shook her head. "I'm a pure soul. Demons are drawn to my light. I didn't want to burden you."

Emethy placed a reassuring hand on Lyra's shoulder. "We're in this together," she said firmly. "No more secrets."

Lyra nodded, her eyes filled with gratitude. Together, they continued their journey, the bond between them growing stronger with each step. As they ventured further towards the old kingdom, Emethy couldn't shake the feeling that the encounter with the demon was just the beginning of the challenges they would face. Yet, she felt a renewed sense of determination, bolstered by the light within her and the spirit by her side.

When they finally stopped to rest, Emethy examined her injuries. The demon had inflicted several deep wounds, but she knew that her body could heal itself with the aid of the moonlight. She lay beneath the night sky, allowing the soothing light to work its magic, and by morning, her wounds had begun to close.

As they prepared to move forward on their journey, Emethy felt a sense of anticipation for what lay ahead. The old kingdom awaited them, and with it, the answers she sought.

And so, with the path ahead shrouded in mystery and danger, Emethy and Lyra moved forward, their journey just beginning.

Chapter 4

The Kingdom's Threshold

The woodland and meadows gave way to undulating hills and busy roads as Emethy and Lyra traveled for days. Each step brought them closer to the fabled kingdom where Seraphina resided, the keeper of ancient lore who could unlock the secrets of the scripture. As they approached the outskirts of the kingdom, a grand structure loomed in the distance—the kingdom's entry door, heavily guarded and imposing.

The walls of the kingdom rose high, their stone surfaces etched with the history and artistry of ages past. Banners fluttered in the breeze, their colors vivid against the gray stone. As they drew nearer, Emethy could see the guards stationed at the gates, their eyes vigilant and their weapons ready.

Lyra floated closer to Emethy, her form shimmering with a mix of excitement and apprehension. "There are so many people inside," she whispered, her voice tinged with awe.

Emethy nodded, her eyes scanning the bustling scene beyond the gates. Merchants haggled with customers, children played in the streets, and townsfolk went about their daily lives. It was a world far removed from the quiet, solitary life she had known in **Elderglen**.

"We need to be careful," Emethy said, her voice low and firm. "They'll be suspicious of us, especially with how we're dressed."

Lyra nodded, understanding the need for caution. Emethy's forest garb, practical and worn, would stand out amid the finely dressed townsfolk and merchants. They needed a plan to blend in, to move through the kingdom without drawing attention.

Emethy led Lyra down a narrow, winding pathway that veered away from the main gates. The alleyways were a labyrinth of shadows and secrets, offering them a chance to observe and strategize. As they walked, Emethy's keen eyes caught sight of a clothesline strung between two buildings, laden with garments left out to dry.

"Stay here," Emethy instructed Lyra, her voice barely a whisper. With practiced stealth, she moved towards the clothesline, her movements swift and silent. She selected a simple yet elegant dress, its fabric soft and flowing, and quickly donned it over her own clothes. The transformation was striking—where once stood a forest girl, now stood a young woman of the kingdom, her appearance befitting the bustling streets and marketplaces.

Emethystin rejoined Lyra, who giggled with delight at the sight. "You look beautiful!" Lyra exclaimed, her spirit flickering with joy.

Emethy couldn't help but smile at Lyra's reaction. "Let's hope this works," she said, adjusting the dress. Together, they made their way back towards the main gates, mingling with a crowd of travellers and merchants entering the kingdom.

The guards at the gate cast wary glances at the newcomers, their eyes sharp and discerning. Emethy kept her head down, her heart pounding in her chest as they approached. She felt Lyra's reassuring presence beside her, a silent reminder of the strength and courage that had brought them this far.

As they passed through the gates, the kingdom unfurled before them like a tapestry of vibrant life. The streets were lined with colourful stalls, their wares ranging from exotic spices to intricate jewellery. The air was filled with the scents of freshly baked bread and roasting meats, mingling with the sounds of laughter and lively conversation.

Lyra floated above Emethy, her eyes wide with wonder. "This place is amazing!" she exclaimed, her voice a mixture of awe and excitement.

Emethy allowed herself a moment of satisfaction. They had made it inside the kingdom, a crucial step towards finding Seraphina and unlocking the secrets of the scripture. The kingdom was a place of beauty and mystery, its streets teeming with life and its buildings standing as silent witnesses to centuries of history.

As they ventured deeper into the kingdom, Emethy couldn't shake the feeling of being watched. The crowds pressed around them, a sea of faces and voices that seemed to blend into a single, overwhelming presence. She kept her senses alert, aware that danger could lurk behind any corner.

"We need to find a place to stay," Emethy said, her voice steady. "Somewhere we can plan our next move and figure out how to find Seraphina."

Lyra nodded, her eyes still wide with curiosity. "There are so many people here," she said, her voice filled with wonder. "How will we find her?"

Emethy glanced around, her mind racing. The kingdom was vast, its streets and alleys a maze of possibilities. "We'll start by asking around," she said. "Someone must know where to find her."

They made their way through the crowded streets, moving with purpose but careful not to draw attention. Emethy's eyes were constantly scanning their surroundings, taking in every detail and assessing every potential threat. She felt a sense of unease, a nagging worry that something—or someone—was watching them.

After several hours of navigating the kingdom's bustling streets, they found a small inn tucked away in a quiet corner. The inn was modest but clean, its owner a kindly old woman who greeted them with a warm smile.

"Welcome, travelers," she said, her voice kind and inviting. "What brings you to our kingdom?"

Emethy hesitated for a moment before responding. "We're looking for someone," she said carefully. "A woman named Seraphina. She's said to be a keeper of ancient lore."

The innkeeper's eyes widened slightly at the mention of Seraphina. "Ah, Seraphina," she said, her voice lowering to a conspiratorial whisper. "She's a recluse, lives in the old quarter near the library. Not many people see her, but she's known for her wisdom and knowledge."

Emethy nodded, feeling a sense of relief. They had a lead, a direction to follow. "Thank you," she said sincerely. "We'll rest here for the night and continue our search in the morning."

The innkeeper smiled and showed them to a small room at the back of the inn. It was simple but comfortable, with a bed and a small table by the window. Emethy thanked the innkeeper again and closed the door, feeling a sense of exhaustion settle over her.

As Emethy and Lyra settled into the room, the weight of their journey began to take its toll. Emethy's body ached from the long days of travel, her mind weary from the constant vigilance. She lay down on the bed, feeling the soft mattress beneath her, and allowed herself a moment of rest.

Lyra floated nearby, her presence a comforting light in the dimly lit room. "We did it, Emethy," she said softly. "We're one step closer."

Emethy nodded, her eyes closing as sleep began to claim her. "Yes," she murmured. "One step closer."

In the quiet moments before sleep, Lyra spoke again, her voice a soft murmur. "You know, Emethy, I haven't slept since my death. It's strange, but I feel at peace when I'm with you."

Emethy opened her eyes briefly, a small smile playing on her lips. "Thank you, Lyra. For being here."

As the first light of dawn began to filter through the window, Emethy awoke with a renewed sense of purpose. Today, they would find Seraphina and uncover the secrets of the scripture. She dressed quickly, her movements efficient and practiced, and prepared herself for the day ahead.

Lyra was already awake, her spirit flickering with anticipation. "Are you ready?" she asked, her voice filled with excitement.

Emethy nodded, a determined look in her eyes. "Let's go," she said.

They made their way through the kingdom's streets once more, following the innkeeper's directions towards the old quarter. The buildings here were older, their stone facades worn by time but still standing strong. The library loomed ahead, a grand structure that seemed to pulse with the weight of knowledge and history.

As they approached the library, Emethy felt a sense of anticipation. This was the moment they had been working towards, the culmination of their journey. She took a deep breath and stepped inside, the cool air and the scent of old books enveloping her.

The library was vast, its shelves filled with ancient tomes and scrolls. Emethy's eyes scanned the room, searching for any sign of Seraphina. Finally, in a quiet corner, she saw an old woman hunched over a table, her eyes focused on a book in front of her.

"Seraphina?" Emethy called softly, her voice hesitant.

The old woman looked up, her eyes sharp and filled with wisdom. "Yes?" she replied, her voice gentle but firm.

Emethy stepped forward, her heart pounding in her chest. "I'm Emethy. I've come to seek your help with a scripture I found. It's said to contain ancient knowledge."

Seraphina's eyes widened as she took in Emethy's words. "Let me see it," she said, her voice filled with curiosity.

Emethy reached into her bag and pulled out the ancient book, handing it to Seraphina. The old woman's eyes widened as she took the book, her fingers tracing the intricate patterns on its cover.

"This is a powerful artifact," Seraphina said, her voice filled with reverence. "It holds knowledge from a time long forgotten. But its secrets are not easily unlocked."

Emethy nodded, feeling a sense of awe. "Can you help us understand it?"

Seraphina looked at Emethy, her eyes filled with wisdom. "I can," she said. "But the journey to uncover its secrets will not be easy. You will face many challenges, and the path will be fraught with danger."

Emethy's expression hardened with determination. "I am ready," she said firmly. "I've come this far, and we won't turn back now."

Seraphina nodded, a small smile playing on her lips. "Very well," she said. "I will help you. But first, there is something you must know."

Emethy leaned in, her curiosity piqued. "What is it?"

Seraphina's expression grew serious. "I am Seraphina, the wife of Emore. Many years ago, I was arrested by the king's order for hiding scriptures of dark possession. I did not have bad intentions—I only wanted to save the world from the dangers these spells could bring."

Emethy's eyes widened in shock. "You were arrested? Why?"

Seraphina sighed, her eyes filled with sorrow. "The king believed I was a threat, that I could use the spells for evil.

But I only wanted to protect the world from those who would misuse them."

Emethy felt a surge of determination. "We'll find a way to clear your name and uncover the secrets of the scripture."

Seraphina smiled, her eyes filled with hope. "Thank you, Emethy. Your courage and determination are truly remarkable."

The next day, Emethy awoke with a sense of purpose. She dressed quickly and retrieved the scripture, determined to learn more about its secrets. But when she reached Seraphina's usual spot in the library, the old woman was nowhere to be found.

Panic surged through Emethy as she asked the librarian if they had seen Seraphina. "She was arrested," the librarian said quietly. "Taken by the king's guards."

Emethy's heart sank, but her resolve only grew stronger. She knew Seraphina could not be guilty of any wrongdoing. She had to find a way to save her.

With a steely determination, Emethy made her way to the royal palace, her mind racing with plans. She would climb the walls if she had to, face any danger that came her way. Seraphina's freedom depended on it.

As Emethy approached the palace, the sun began to set, casting long shadows across the grounds. She took a deep breath, her mind focused on the task ahead.

"Seraphina will be saved," she whispered to herself. "I won't let her suffer for trying to protect the world."

With that, she began to climb, her movements swift and sure. The challenges ahead were daunting, but Emethy knew she could face them. For Seraphina, for the secrets of the scripture, and for the future they sought to protect.

Quote: *"In the face of darkness, it is our courage that lights the way, guiding us towards the truth and the justice we seek."*

Chapter 5

The Prince & The Secret

Emethy's hands grasped the cold stone of the palace wall as she hoisted herself up, her heart pounding with determination. The palace loomed above her, its grandeur and vastness overwhelming. The sprawling gardens and intricate architecture spoke of wealth and power,

but Emethy had no time to marvel at the sights. Her focus was on finding Seraphina and uncovering the secrets of the scripture.

As she navigated the labyrinthine corridors and lush gardens of the palace, Emethy couldn't shake the feeling of being watched. She moved with the stealth and agility she had honed in the forest, slipping through shadows and avoiding the notice of guards and servants.

One evening, as she explored a secluded part of the garden, she encountered a young man. He was standing by a fountain, his expression contemplative. Emethy's first instinct was to retreat, but curiosity held her in place.

The man was handsome, with a kind face and an air of quiet strength. Lyra, invisible to everyone but Emethy, hovered nearby and whispered, "He's handsome, Emethy. You should approach him."

Emethy shook her head slightly, her determination unwavering. "I'm not here for distractions," she whispered back. "We need to find Seraphina."

The young man turned at the sound of her voice, his eyes meeting hers. "Hello," he said, his voice gentle. "I haven't seen you around before. Are you new here?"

Emethy hesitated, choosing her words carefully. "Yes, I'm... new. Just trying to find my way."

The young man smiled, a warm and genuine smile that reached his eyes. "I'm Alaric. And you are?"

"Emethy," she replied, her voice steady but guarded.

"Well, Emethy, if you need any help, feel free to ask," Alaric said. "The palace can be quite overwhelming at first."

Emethy nodded, but her mind was already racing with thoughts of Seraphina and the scripture. She couldn't afford to get too close to anyone, not now.

As the days turned into weeks, Emethy settled into a routine. During the day, she worked in the kingdom, blending in with the other workers and gathering information. In the evenings, she returned to the palace, continuing her search for Seraphina. She discovered that Alaric was not just any young man but the prince—the son of the king. Despite this revelation, she kept her distance, her focus unwavering.

Alaric, for his part, noticed Emethy's presence more and more. He saw her moving through the gardens, her eyes always scanning her surroundings with an intensity that intrigued him. One evening, as she was about to leave, he approached her again.

"You're very dedicated," he said, his voice breaking the silence.

Emethy turned to face him, her expression neutral. "I have a lot to do."

Alaric nodded, his eyes searching hers. "I understand. My mother was the same way. She was a healer, you know. Very skilled, like you."

Emethy's heart skipped a beat at the mention of his mother. "She sounds remarkable."

"She was," Alaric said softly. "She passed away when I was young, but I remember how she used to care for everyone. She had a gentle touch, much like yours."

Emethy felt a pang of sorrow, but she quickly pushed it aside. "I'm sorry for your loss."

"Thank you," Alaric replied. "You remind me of her in many ways. You have the same strength and determination."

Emethy remained silent, not trusting herself to respond. She felt a connection to Alaric, a shared understanding of loss and responsibility, but she couldn't afford to let it distract her.

As the weeks went by, Emethy's search for Seraphina grew more desperate. She scoured every corner of the palace, following leads and piecing together clues. Each evening, she returned to the gardens, hoping for a breakthrough.

One night, as she was searching a particularly remote part of the palace, Alaric found her again. "Emethy, I've been thinking," he said, his voice serious. "There's something you're not telling me."

Emethy's heart raced, but she kept her expression calm. "I don't know what you mean."

Alaric stepped closer, his eyes intense. "I've seen the way you move, the way you search. You're not just a maid. You're looking for something—someone."

Emethy's breath caught in her throat. She couldn't deny it any longer. "I'm looking for Seraphina," she admitted. "She was arrested, and I need to find her."

Alaric's eyes widened in surprise. "Seraphina? The king's prisoner?"

"Yes," Emethy said, her voice firm. "She holds the key to something very important. I need to find her before it's too late."

Alaric looked at her for a long moment, his expression thoughtful. "I can help you," he said finally. "But you have to trust me."

Emethy hesitated, torn between her need for help and her instinct to keep her mission secret. Finally, she nodded. "Okay. I'll trust you."

Together, they devised a plan. Alaric would use his position to gain access to restricted areas of the palace, while Emethy would continue to search and gather information. They worked side by side, their partnership growing stronger with each passing day.

As they searched, Lyra remained a constant presence, her spirit flickering with excitement and curiosity. She giggled at Alaric's attempts to impress Emethy, her light-heartedness a stark contrast to Emethy's intensity.

One evening, as they were poring over a map of the palace, Alaric spoke again. "My mother once told me about a secret passageway in the palace," he said. "It was used during times of war to move people in and out undetected. If Seraphina is being held somewhere, that passageway might be our best chance to find her."

Emethy's eyes lit up with hope. "Where is it?"

Alaric pointed to a spot on the map, a hidden entrance near the east wing. "It's here. We'll have to be careful, though. It's heavily guarded."

Emethy nodded, her determination renewed. "We'll make it work. We have to."

With Alaric's help, Emethy navigated the secret passageway, her heart pounding with anticipation. The narrow corridor was dark and musty, the air thick with the scent of age and neglect. They moved silently, their footsteps echoing softly against the stone walls.

As they neared the end of the passageway, they heard voices. Emethy's heart raced as she strained to listen, her senses alert. She could hear the guards talking, their voices muffled but distinct.

"We need to be quiet," Alaric whispered, his voice barely audible. "Follow me."

They crept forward, their movements slow and deliberate. Alaric led the way, his familiarity with the palace guiding them through the labyrinthine corridors. Finally, they reached a small, hidden door.

"This is it," Alaric said softly. "She's in there."

Emethy took a deep breath, her hand resting on the door handle. She glanced at Alaric, who nodded reassuringly. With a steadying breath, she pushed the door open.

Inside, the room was dimly lit, its air heavy with the scent of herbs and old books. In the center of the room, bound and weary, was Seraphina. Her eyes widened in surprise as she saw Emethy and Alaric.

"Emethy?" Seraphina's voice was hoarse, her expression a mix of relief and disbelief. "How did you find me?"

"We didn't give up," Emethy said, her voice filled with determination. "We're here to get you out."

Alaric moved to untie Seraphina, his movements quick and efficient. "We have to hurry," he said. "The guards will notice she's gone soon."

As they worked to free Seraphina, Emethy felt a surge of hope. They were so close—so close to uncovering the secrets of the scripture and saving Seraphina. But their journey was far from over.

Once Seraphina was free, they made their way back through the secret passageway, moving quickly and silently. The palace seemed to close in around them, its corridors a maze of shadows and danger.

As they emerged into the garden, Emethy felt a sense of relief. They had made it this far, but there was still much to do. She turned to Seraphina, her expression serious.

"We need to find a safe place," she said. "Somewhere we can learn more about the scripture and plan our next move."

Seraphina nodded, her eyes filled with gratitude. "Thank you, Emethy. I knew you would find me."

Emethy felt a warmth spread through her chest at Seraphina's words. They had come so far, and there was still much to uncover. But for now, they had each other—and the determination to see their mission through.

Quote: *"In the heart of the storm, it is our unwavering determination that becomes the beacon of hope, guiding us through the darkest of times."*

Chapter 6

Secrets In the Moonlight

The moon hung high in the star-speckled sky, casting a silvery veil over the palace gardens. The night air was cold and crisp, heavy with the scent of damp earth and blooming nightshade. Emethystin, Alaric, and Seraphina made their way to a secluded part of the garden, a place of tranquillity away from the palace's usual bustle. Seraphina, still weak and shivering, leaned heavily on Emethy, her pallid face drawn in pain and exhaustion.

They carefully laid Seraphina down on a makeshift bed of soft leaves and blankets beneath the protective cover of an ancient oak. The moonlight filtered through the canopy, dappling their surroundings in gentle, ethereal light. Emethy's heart ached as she saw Seraphina's frail condition. She knew that urgent care was needed.

"We need to treat her immediately," Emethy instructed, her voice steady despite the worry churning inside her.

She set to work with practiced efficiency, gathering herbs and natural remedies from the small satchel she always carried. Her fingers worked deftly, preparing poultices and balms with careful precision.

Alaric stood nearby, his gaze fixed on Emethystin with a mixture of admiration and concern. He looked at her with eyes that reflected both his respect for her skill and his worry for Seraphina. "Is there anything I can do to help?" he asked, his voice filled with earnestness.

Emethy glanced up, her eyes meeting his with a hint of gratitude. "Fetch some water and find more blankets. She needs to stay warm."

Alaric nodded, his face set with determination. He hurried off into the shadows, returning soon with a bucket of fresh water and several blankets. Together, they worked to make Seraphina as comfortable as possible. Emethy applied the poultices to Seraphina's wounds, her touch both gentle and firm.

As the hours passed, the soft murmur of the night was punctuated only by the rhythmic rustling of leaves and the occasional hoot of an owl. Seraphina's breathing grew steadier, her color slowly returning. Emethy sat back, wiping the sweat from her brow, and took a deep breath. "She'll need time to recover fully, but she's stable for now."

Alaric, sitting beside her, looked at her with unspoken admiration. "You're amazing, Emethy. The way you care for others... it's remarkable."

Emethy felt a warmth spread through her chest at his words, a rare sensation that had been absent from her life for so long. "Thank you," she said softly, her voice tinged with genuine appreciation.

The night was still, but the air between her and Prince Alaric buzzed with a tension neither could ignore. She could feel his eyes on her, a heat that burned through the cool night air. She had kept him at a distance for so long, but now, with the weight of her journey pressing down on her, she found herself drawn to him in ways she had never allowed herself before.

Alaric stepped closer, his hand brushing against hers, sending a shiver down her spine. She turned to face him, her heart pounding in her chest. His gaze was intense, his eyes searching hers as if seeking permission for what they both knew was about to happen.

"Emethy," he whispered, his voice low and rough with emotion. He lifted a hand to her cheek, his thumb tracing the line of her jaw. She leaned into his touch, her breath hitching as he closed the distance between them. The sensation was interrupted only by the subtle presence of Lyra, who, sensing the moment, floated away to give them privacy.

Before she could think, before she could remind herself of all the reasons this was dangerous, his lips were on hers. The kiss was slow at first, testing, tasting, but the moment her lips parted, it deepened, igniting something fierce between them. His hands slid down her back, pulling her closer, and she could feel the strength in his arms, the desire that matched her own.

Emethy's hands found their way to his chest, feeling the rapid beat of his heart beneath his tunic. She clutched at the fabric, losing herself in the warmth of his embrace, in the way he made her feel alive, as if the world outside the window no longer mattered.

As his lips trailed down her neck, pressing kisses against her skin, Emethy gasped, her head tilting back in surrender. But then, his hand moved lower, slipping beneath the fabric of her tunic, fingers brushing against the skin of her shoulder.

The tension between them eased, replaced by a quiet intimacy. Alaric reached out, brushing a stray strand of hair from Emethy's face. Their eyes met, and in that moment, the world around them seemed to fade away. Slowly, tentatively, Alaric leaned in and pressed his lips to hers.

The kiss was soft and tender, a connection of souls amidst the chaos that had enveloped them. Emethy felt a rush of emotions—relief, desire, and a burgeoning hope she hadn't allowed herself to feel in a long time.

But as the clouds parted and the full moon cast its light upon them, Emethy's birthmark began to glow through her dress. Alaric pulled back, his eyes widening in shock. "Emethy... What's that?" he asked, his voice a mixture of curiosity and confusion.

Panic flared in Emethy's chest. She pulled away, turning her back to him, her hand covering the mark as if she could hide it from his view. "It's nothing," she said, her voice trembling despite her efforts to sound strong.

Emethy hesitated, her heart sinking as she turned slightly to reveal the mark. "It's a birthmark. It glows under the full moon."

Alaric's expression shifted from surprise to something darker—anger. "I've heard stories about such marks. They're said to be a sign of dark magic or a curse."

Emethy's heart sank further at his words. "It's not a curse," she insisted, her voice rising in defence. "I don't know what it means, but it's not evil."

Without another word, Alaric stood abruptly and walked away, leaving Emethy alone in the moonlit shade. She felt a deep sense of loss and confusion, but she forced herself to focus on Seraphina's recovery.

When Emethy returned to Seraphina, the spirit of Lyra hovered nearby, her presence a constant source of comfort. Lyra's eyes were filled with concern. "Emethy, what happened?" she asked, her voice filled with worry.

Emethy shook her head, not trusting herself to speak. She busied herself with tending to Seraphina, pushing aside the ache in her heart. Lyra, sensing her distress, remained close, her silent support a small solace.

Days passed, and Alaric did not return. Emethy's hope dwindled as each day wore on, and she found herself growing more distant from those around her. Lyra did her best to cheer Emethy up, but the weight of Alaric's absence and the fear of their mission's failure kept Emethy's heart heavy.

One morning, as the first light of dawn crept over the horizon, Seraphina stirred and began to read from the ancient scripture they had recovered. Her voice was weak but determined, each word a labor of effort. "This text speaks of death," she said, her eyes scanning the faded pages. "A force that comes for everyone, unstoppable and inevitable."

Emethy felt a chill run down her spine. She had witnessed so much death in her life—friends, neighbors, those she had loved and lost. She hated death with a passion that burned like a cold fire. "Is there anything about how to stop it?" she asked, her voice barely above a whisper.

Seraphina shook her head, her brow furrowed with concentration. "It doesn't say. But there is more to this text. I need time to decipher it."

Just as Seraphina was about to continue, Lyra appeared, her face pale with worry. "Emethy, guards are coming. We have to leave now!"

Emethy's heart raced as panic surged through her. They quickly gathered their belongings, and Emethy supported Seraphina as they fled the secluded shade. They moved as swiftly as their circumstances allowed, but Seraphina's weakened state hampered their progress.

As they reached the edge of the palace grounds, Emethy's mind raced with anger and betrayal. She couldn't shake the feeling that Alaric had somehow betrayed them, though she knew he might not have been aware of the guards' pursuit. Her gaze flickered back at the palace, her heart heavy with suspicion and unresolved emotions.

Little did she know, Alaric was not aware of the guards' pursuit. His absence was not the result of treachery but rather his own inner turmoil. As Emethy and her companions disappeared into the night, Alaric stood at the palace window, his thoughts consumed by the girl with the glowing mark. He wrestled with his conflicted feelings, his mind torn between duty and a growing, unspoken concern for Emethy.

The moon continued its journey across the sky, indifferent to the human dramas unfolding below. Emethy and her companions vanished into the darkness, their fate uncertain, while the palace remained a place of shadows and unanswered questions.

Emethy sat by the flickering fire, the night air cool against her skin. The forest around her was quiet, save for the soft rustle of leaves in the breeze. Lyra was asleep, curled up beside her, but Emethy's mind was far from rest. She stared into the flames, her thoughts drifting to Prince Alaric, the man she had met only once, yet couldn't seem to forget.

She sighed, her voice barely above a whisper as she spoke to herself. "Prince Alaric... What is it about you that lingers in my mind? I've faced demons and spirits, seen death more times than I can count, yet it's your eyes that haunt me. Those eyes... they seemed to see right through me, as if you knew the weight I carry, the secrets I keep."

She paused, the crackling of the fire filling the silence. "You live in a world of power and privilege, surrounded by walls and Guards. But when you looked at me, it felt like you understood. You didn't see just a healer, a girl from the woods—you saw me, Emethy, with all my fears, my anger, my pain."

Her heart ached with a longing she didn't want to acknowledge. "I can't let myself feel this way. I can't afford to care for someone like you. I've seen too much, lost too many. If I let you in... what would that mean for me? For this path I'm on?"

Emethy closed her eyes, trying to push the thoughts away. But they persisted, as stubborn as she was. "You're a prince, and I am... well, I'm not meant for anything more than what I have to do. But still, I wonder... in another life, another time, could there have been a chance for us? Or is this just another dream, destined to fade with the morning light?"

She opened her eyes and gazed at the sky, where the stars twinkled, indifferent to the turmoil in her heart. "Maybe it's better this way. Maybe it's better that you remain just a memory, a fleeting thought in the quiet of the night. Because if I ever let myself feel more... I don't know if I could ever turn back."

Emethy sighed deeply, as if trying to release the weight of her emotions into the night air. "But even if I try to forget you, Prince Alaric, I know a part of me will always remember. Because you were the first to look at me and see more than what I show the world. And maybe... maybe that's something I'll hold onto, even when everything else fades away."

Emethy whispered to the wind, her voice heavy with sorrow, "I have to leave you behind, Prince Alaric. Not because I want to, but because I must. My path was forged long before you stepped into it, and as much as my heart aches to stay, I know I can't. I'll carry the memory of you with me, like a secret tucked away in the quietest corners of my soul. But I have to let you go, for your sake and mine, even if it means leaving a piece of my heart behind with you."

Emethy moved through the dense forest with Seraphina and Lyra by her side. The oppressive canopy above cast shifting shadows on the forest floor, and the muffled whisper of the trees seemed to speak in hushed, ancient tones. The dark forest stretched endlessly ahead, a labyrinth of twisting roots and tangled underbrush. The air was thick with the scent of earth and pine, and the occasional call of a distant creature echoed through the gloom. Lyra floated beside Emethy, her translucent form emitting a faint, soothing glow that cut through the darkness like a beacon of hope.

"We need to find a place to rest and plan our next move," Emethy said, her voice steady despite the exhaustion creeping into her bones. Her eyes were bloodshot, and her steps were growing heavier with each mile they covered.

Seraphina, the former queen whose arrest had marked the end of an era, nodded thoughtfully. Her once regal bearing now carried a weariness that spoke of both her fall from grace and the burden of her own choices. "There is a castle not far from here," she said, her voice a soft murmur against the backdrop of the forest's sighs. "It's a place of safety and mystery, and its owner is someone I trust."

Emethy's gaze sharpened with renewed focus. "Lead the way."

As they ventured deeper into the forest, the oppressive darkness began to lift, revealing a faint, mesmerizing glow that seemed to beckon them forward. Emethy quickened her pace, her heart quickening with a mixture of hope and apprehension. The ethereal light grew brighter, and as they emerged from the thick canopy, they found themselves standing before a castle bathed in the soft hues of twilight. The structure shimmered as if made of moonlight itself, with elegant towers piercing the sky and stone walls covered with climbing ivy that glowed faintly in the moon's silver embrace.

"This place is enchanting," Lyra whispered, her voice filled with awe. Her eyes, usually so full of mischief and curiosity, were now wide with wonder.

Emethy nodded, her own gaze scanning the surroundings with a mixture of caution and relief. "Let's hope whoever lives here is as welcoming as the castle appears."

Chapter 7

The Dim light Castle

The castle loomed ahead, shrouded in eerie silence, as their cautious footsteps sank into the overgrown moss carpeting the forgotten path. The grand doors creaked open as if stirred by an unseen force, revealing a tall, graceful woman standing in the entryway. Her presence was commanding yet mysterious, imbued with an air of wisdom and latent power.

She appeared to be in her thirties, with an ageless beauty that seemed both timeless and otherworldly. Her serene demeanor contrasted sharply with the world outside, and beside her stood a sleek black cat with a peculiar, crescent-shaped mark on its back. The cat's piercing eyes seemed to hold an unfathomable depth, watching them with an unsettling awareness.

"Welcome," the lady said softly, her voice like a melodious whisper that seemed to resonate with the very walls of the castle. "You seem weary from your travels. Please, come in and rest."

Emethy hesitated for a moment, her instincts at war with her exhaustion. Yet the warmth emanating from within, along with the faint scent of herbs that wafted through the open door, proved irresistible. She stepped inside, and Lyra followed closely, though the black cat's unblinking gaze made the spirit fidget uncomfortably.

"Thank you," Emethy replied, her voice tinged with cautious gratitude. "We appreciate your kindness."

The lady led them to a cozy room with a fireplace crackling warmly in the hearth. The room was ith decorated w an assortment of tapestries and artifacts that hinted at a life of both comfort and mystery. The lady gestured to a table laden with bread and cheese, along with a steaming pot of herbal tea. "You may call me Althea," she said, her eyes lingering on Emethy with an intensity that suggested she was trying to decipher a puzzle. "Make yourselves at home."

As they settled in, Emethy couldn't shake the feeling of being scrutinized. The cat's gaze was unwavering, as though it were trying to pierce through the very essence of Lyra. The spirit, usually so carefree, seemed unnerved.

"The cat can sense me," Lyra murmured, her voice barely audible. She floated closer to Emethy, seeking solace in her proximity.

Althea's eyes flickered briefly toward Lyra, but she remained poised and composed, as if she hadn't noticed the spirit at all. Instead, she offered Emethy and Seraphina the food with a graceful nod.

"Thank you," Emethy said, accepting the bread and cheese with a gratitude that was genuine. She hadn't realized how hungry she was until the simple meal was set before her, and each bite felt like a small piece of comfort in an otherwise tumultuous journey.

As they ate, Lyra floated closer to Emethy, her voice a soft whisper. "You know, Emethy, you resemble Althea quite a bit. It's almost like looking at an older version of you."

Emethy frowned, her brow furrowing as she chewed thoughtfully. "I am my own person. I don't want to feel connected to anyone."

Althea watched them with an enigmatic smile, her expression a mask of serene detachment. She spoke only when necessary, her words measured and wise, leaving much unsaid.

Days turned into weeks, and Emethy grew accustomed to the serene life within the castle's walls. Althea's presence was quietly intriguing, her extensive knowledge of herbs and healing proving invaluable. Yet, beneath the calm façade, there was an unspoken tension, a sense that Althea knew more about Emethy than she was willing to share. The castle itself seemed to whisper secrets through its creaking timbers and shifting shadows.

One evening, as they sat by the fire, its flickering light casting dancing shadows on the walls, Althea spoke in hushed tones. "The scripture you seek is related to an ancient power, one born of darkness and destined to rise as an empress. But without the complete scripture, the full truth remains hidden."

Emethy's eyes widened with a mix of surprise and resolve. "The other half is in the king's palace. I need to find it."

Althea nodded solemnly. "Be cautious, Emethy. The path you walk is fraught with danger."

As the days passed, Emethy's resolve only hardened. She was determined to retrieve the remaining part of the scripture. Seraphina, always the voice of wisdom and experience, guided her through the ancient texts and stories, sharing knowledge about the ancient powers and their potential dangers.

One night, as the wind howled outside and the castle seemed to hold its breath, Seraphina spoke with a somber tone. "Emethy, the scripture speaks of a power that can only be wielded by someone born in darkness. An empress with the strength to command the shadows."

Emethy listened intently, her curiosity piqued and her determination solidified. "What does that mean for us? For me?"

"It means that your journey is far from over," Seraphina replied gently. "But with the other half of the scripture, we can uncover the full extent of its power and the role you are meant to play."

Emethy nodded, the weight of her destiny pressing down on her like a tangible force. "I will find the other half, no matter what it takes."

Emethystin prepared to set out towards the kingdom, a chilling presence emerged from the shadows. A creature, its form twisted by rage and sorrow, lurched toward her with a guttural snarl.

"Why do you tread upon my domain?" the creature demanded, its voice a harsh rasp.

Emethy drew her sword, her heart pounding with adrenaline. "I have no quarrel with you, but I will defend myself."

The battle that ensued was fierce and unrelenting. The creature's movements were erratic and filled with a frenzied anger that pushed Emethystin to her limits. Her sword flashed in the moonlight as she parried and struck with all her strength. Each clash of steel against claw echoed through the night, and Emethy's determination was the only thing that kept her from succumbing to exhaustion.

Despite her valiant efforts, a blow to her shoulder sent her staggering. With a final, desperate surge of energy, she drove her sword into the creature's side. It let out a pained roar that reverberated through the forest before collapsing, its body convulsing in its death throes.

Emethy, breathing heavily and covered in sweat and blood, approached the fallen creature cautiously. "Why are you so angry?" she demanded, her voice rough with emotion.

The creature's eyes dimmed, and the fury gave way to profound sorrow. "My daughter... a human killed her and trapped her spirit. I am cursed with her pain."

Emethy's heart ached with sympathy for the creature's tragic plight. "I am sorry for your loss. May you find peace."

With a heavy heart, she turned back towards the castle, her steps faltering with exhaustion and grief. Althea awaited her at the entrance, her expression unreadable as she offered Emethy medicinal herbs and assisted her in tending to her wounds.

"You encountered a creature," Althea stated, her tone neutral but carrying an undercurrent of concern.

Emethy nodded, wincing as she applied the herbs. "It was filled with sorrow and rage. I... I had to fight it."

Lyra hovered nearby, her eyes wide with concern and a touch of fear. "Emethy, are you alright?"

Emethy forced a smile, though it didn't reach her eyes. "I'm fine, Lyra. Just a little bruised."

As Emethy rested, Althea sat silently, her gaze distant. The fire crackled, casting long shadows that danced on the stone walls. Emethy couldn't shake the feeling that Althea knew more about her journey than she revealed. But for now, Emethystin was grateful for the sanctuary and the enigmatic presence of Althea, who seemed to be a guardian of secrets in this dimly lit castle.

Lyra, however, remained troubled. "Emethy, I'm worried. That creature... there might be more like it."

Emethy nodded, the weight of her responsibility pressing heavily on her. "I know. But we have to keep moving forward. We need to find the rest of the scripture."

With renewed determination, Emethy resolved to uncover the truth, knowing that her path was intertwined with ancient powers and dark secrets. The road ahead was perilous, but she was ready to face whatever challenges lay in wait, guided by the mysterious presence of Althea and the unwavering spirit of Lyra by her side.

Quote: "True strength lies not in the absence of fear, but in the resolve to face it, no matter the cost."

Chapter 8

The Other Half of the Scripture & Lost Lyra

Emethystin walked deliberately, taking slow, deliberate steps. She had left the safety of the dim light castle, determined to retrieve the remaining half of the scripture. Beside her, Lyra's ghostly form hovered, a silent companion on this perilous journey.

"We must be careful, Emethy," Lyra whispered, her voice barely audible above the rustling leaves. "The king is not to be underestimated."

Emethy nodded, her resolve unwavering. "I know, Lyra. But we need that scripture to uncover the truth."

As they approached the palace, Emethy's heart pounded with anticipation. The grand structure loomed before them, its towering spires reaching toward the heavens. Shadows danced along the walls, and the air was thick with an unsettling energy. The guards patrolled the perimeter, their eyes sharp and their weapons at the ready.

"We need to find a way in," Emethy murmured, scanning the area for any possible entrance.

Lyra pointed to a small, unguarded door on the side of the palace. "There. We can slip in through there."

Emethy nodded and moved swiftly, her movements silent and precise. They reached the door, and with a gentle push, it creaked open. Inside, the palace was dimly lit, the flickering torches casting eerie shadows along the stone walls.

They moved through the corridors, keeping to the shadows to avoid detection. The palace was a maze of hallways and chambers, each more opulent than the last. Emethy's heart raced as they passed by the rooms of nobles and officials, their opulent decor a stark contrast to the grim task at hand.

"We need to find the library," Emethy whispered, her eyes scanning the corridors for any sign of their destination.

After what felt like an eternity, they found it: an immense, grand library filled with rows upon rows of ancient tomes and scrolls. The air was thick with the scent of aged parchment and dust, and the silence was almost oppressive.

Emethy moved quickly, her eyes darting from shelf to shelf. She searched through countless books, scrolls, and manuscripts, her frustration growing with each passing moment. But the scripture was nowhere to be found.

"Where could it be?" Emethy muttered, her voice tinged with desperation.

As she continued her search, a sound caught her attention. She froze, her heart pounding. From the corner of her eye, she saw a flicker of movement. Emethy turned, her eyes narrowing as she saw a figure moving down a nearby alley.

"Come on, Lyra," Emethy whispered, moving towards the alley. "Let's check it out."

They followed the figure, careful to stay hidden in the shadows. The alley led to a chamber, its entrance adorned with strange symbols and runes. Emethy's breath caught in her throat as she realized where they were.

"This is the king's chamber of rituals," Lyra whispered, her voice filled with awe and fear. "We need to be very careful."

Emethy nodded, her eyes scanning the chamber. The room was filled with strange artifacts, ritualistic tools, and dark tomes. The air was thick with the scent of incense and the faint echo of chanting.

Emethy moved cautiously, her eyes searching for any sign of the scripture. As she approached a large, ornate desk, she saw it: the other half of the scripture, its ancient pages filled with cryptic symbols and writings.

"Lyra, we found it," Emethy whispered, a smile of relief spreading across her face.

But as she reached for the scripture, she realized something was wrong. Lyra was nowhere to be found.

"Lyra?" Emethy called out softly, her heart pounding with panic. "Where are you?"

There was no response. The chamber seemed to grow colder, and the shadows seemed to close in around her. Emethy's hands trembled as she took the scripture and quickly hid it in her satchel. She had to find Lyra and get out of the palace before they were discovered.

She moved swiftly through the corridors, her mind racing. Where could Lyra have gone? Had she been captured? The thought sent a chill down Emethy's spine.

As she turned a corner, she heard a voice call out from behind her, "Who are you?"

Emethy's heart stopped as she turned to see the king himself, his form twisted and malevolent. He moved with a crooked gait, his eyes burning with a dark, unsettling energy.

Before she could respond, a figure stepped out of the shadows. "She's with me, Father."

Emethy blinked in surprise as the prince appeared, his expression calm and composed. "She's a new worker I brought to the palace. She was just lost."

The king's eyes narrowed, suspicion etched into his features. "Is that so?"

The prince nodded, his gaze unwavering. "Yes. I'll take responsibility for her. Come, Emethy."

Emethy followed the prince, her heart racing with a mix of relief and anger. Once they were out of the king's sight, she turned to the prince, her eyes blazing. "Why did you do that? You could have gotten us both killed."

The prince shrugged, a faint smile playing on his lips. "You seemed like you needed help. Besides, it's not safe to wander the palace alone at night."

Emethy clenched her fists, struggling to keep her voice steady. "I didn't need your help. I was looking for someone."

The prince raised an eyebrow. "Who?"

Emethy hesitated, unable to reveal the truth about Lyra. "It doesn't matter. I need to find them."

The prince studied her for a moment, his expression thoughtful. "If you need assistance, you can come to me. But be careful. My father is not as forgiving as I am."

Emethy nodded curtly, her mind still focused on finding Lyra. "Thank you. But I need to go."

She moved quickly, her steps light and purposeful. She had to find Lyra and get out of the palace before the king's suspicions grew. The corridors seemed to stretch on endlessly, each shadow hiding potential danger.

Finally, she heard a faint whisper. "Emethy..."

Emethy turned, her heart sinking. Lyra was still missing. As she retraced her steps, she realized she needed to leave the palace and regroup. The risk of being caught was too high, and the king's presence loomed like a dark cloud.

"I have to go back to the castle," she whispered to herself, feeling a pang of guilt for leaving without finding Lyra. But she couldn't endanger herself further.

She moved stealthily back through the corridors and slipped out the same way she had entered. The night air was cool and crisp, a stark contrast to the oppressive atmosphere inside the palace. Emethy's mind raced with thoughts of Lyra and the scripture. She had to find a way to save her friend and uncover the secrets of the ancient text.

As she made her way back to the dim light castle, Emethy couldn't shake the feeling that the king had something to do with Lyra's disappearance. The memory of his twisted form and burning eyes haunted her thoughts.

"We did it, Lyra," Emethy whispered to the night, hoping her friend could somehow hear her. "We have the scripture. Now we just need to figure out what it means and how to save you."

As she approached the castle, Emethy felt a renewed sense of determination. She wouldn't rest until she had freed Lyra and uncovered the truth hidden within the ancient scripture. The journey ahead would be fraught with danger, but Emethy knew she had the strength and resolve to face whatever challenges lay ahead.

Chapter 9

The Mysterious Althea

Emethy's mind was a storm of thoughts as she returned to the dim light castle. The memory of the book on the podium in the king's chamber, the one about captive spirits, lingered in her mind. She had to rescue Lyra, and quickly.

The moment she entered her room, she placed the ancient scripture in a hidden trunk she had crafted in the floor. She carefully slid the floorboards back into place, ensuring the trunk was well concealed. Only then did she allow herself to breathe a little easier, knowing the precious text was safe.

Dinner that evening was a quiet affair. Emethy and Seraphina sat at the table with Althea, the mysterious owner of the castle, and her enigmatic black cat. The cat, usually aloof and watchful, was surprisingly calm tonight, sitting placidly under the table.

The silence was broken by Althea's unexpected question. "Where is that little girl who is always with you?"

Emethy's hand froze mid-air, a spoonful of soup poised at her lips. Her heart skipped a beat. How did Althea know about Lyra? She had never mentioned the spirit to anyone, especially not in front of Seraphina, who was blissfully unaware of Lyra's existence.

"I... I don't know what you mean," Emethy stammered, trying to maintain her composure. "There's no little girl."

Althea's lips curled into a faint smile, her eyes twinkling with a knowing look. "Of course," she said softly, her gaze lingering on Emethy for a moment before she stood up. "I think I'll retire for the evening. Good night."

Emethy watched as Althea left the room, her mind a whirlwind of confusion and suspicion. How much did Althea know? Could she be trusted?

Seraphina leaned closer, her voice barely above a whisper. "Emethy, is something wrong?"

Emethy shook her head, forcing a smile. "No, nothing at all. Just tired."

After dinner, Emethy decided to take a bath to clear her mind. The warm water helped to relax her muscles, but her thoughts continued to race. How did Althea know about Lyra? And what did she mean by her cryptic question?

As she lay in bed that night, the pieces of the puzzle refused to fit together. Althea was a mystery, and Emethy couldn't afford any distractions from her main goal: rescuing Lyra. But the more she thought about it, the more she realized that Althea's knowledge could be both a danger and an opportunity.

Eventually, exhaustion claimed her, and Emethy drifted into a restless sleep, her dreams filled with images of Lyra, the king's twisted form, and the enigmatic smile of Althea.

In the days that followed, Emethy's resolve only grew stronger. She knew she had to find a way back into the palace and retrieve the book on captive spirits. It held the key to freeing Lyra and possibly many others.

During the daytime, Emethy focused on her plan, mapping out every detail with Seraphina's help. They would need to create a distraction, slip past the guards, and find the book. Emethy couldn't afford any mistakes.

At night, the castle's quiet corridors became a place of reflection and strategy. Emethy often found herself thinking about Althea, her cryptic words, and her seemingly endless well of secrets. The cat, with its knowing green eyes, seemed to follow her every move, as if it too held untold stories.

Emethy knew that the path ahead was fraught with danger, but she had no choice. Lyra needed her, and she would stop at nothing to bring her back. And as for Althea, Emethy would find out the truth in due time. For now, her focus was on the mission at hand.

With a final deep breath, Emethy closed her eyes, allowing herself a moment of rest before the storm she knew was coming. She would need all her strength and cunning for the battle that lay ahead.

For several days Emethy had been silently watching Althea, attempting
to understand the mysterious woman who had taken th

em in. One particularly cold winter night, when Althea went out for her usual evening grocery run, Emethy seized the opportunity to explore Althea's quarters more thoroughly. She had been thorough in her search before, but this time, something new caught her eye: an old, leather-bound book tucked away on a high shelf.

Emethy reached for the book, her fingers trembling with anticipation. As she flipped through its pages, she found detailed instructions on rituals and spells that could free a captive soul. Relief washed over her, and she clutched the book to her chest, feeling a renewed sense of hope. This book could be the key to saving Lyra.

Carefully placing the book back where she found it, Emethy couldn't help but feel a pang of sympathy for Althea. Despite her mysterious nature and distant demeanor, Althea seemed burdened by her own secrets. Her consistent evening routine painted a picture of a woman bound by duty and solitude.

As Emethy made her way back to her room, she heard a soft knock on her window. She peered out and was shocked to see Prince Alaric, disguised as a village boy.

His visit was a significant risk to his identity, and it infuriated Emethy.

She opened the window just enough to confront him. "What are you doing here? You'll get us both killed!" She slammed the window shut, but Alaric didn't leave. He continued to plead with her to come out and talk.

Unable to contain her curiosity and frustration, Emethy slipped out to the back of the castle, the black cat trailing behind her. She pulled Alaric into a shadowy corner, away from prying eyes.

"What do you want?" she demanded, her voice low and fierce. "Why are you here?"

"I had to see you. We need to talk," Alaric replied, his voice tense with urgency.

Emethy's eyes blazed with anger. "Talk about what? How you betrayed us when Seraphina was injured? How you told the king about us?"

Alaric's face flushed with anger and hurt. "I didn't betray you! I told no one about you. The king's Guards are everywhere. I was scared, Emethy! You don't understand what that mark on your body means. I found out about it from the books in the library. It's a mark of the chosen one, a symbol of great power and danger."

Emethy's mark had always been a source of mystery and fear for her, but hearing it called the mark of the chosen one only intensified her rage. "So, you're here because of some prophecy? Because I might be the chosen one? You don't care about me at all!"

"That's not true!" Alaric shouted, his voice echoing through the night. "I care about you, Emethy. But this is bigger than both of us. I didn't know how to handle it."

Emethy's anger didn't subside. "You only care because you're scared of what I might become. You don't see me, just the mark."

Alaric looked away, the pain in his eyes evident. "I'm sorry," he whispered. "I was wrong."

But Emethy couldn't accept his apology. "This is what you do. You run away when things get tough." She turned her back on him, her words cutting through the cold night air.

Emethy watched him go, her heart heavy with a mix of anger and sorrow. She noticed Althea but didn't say anything. Althea, as usual, remained silent, her expression unreadable. She didn't ask Emethy about the argument, her demeanour as cold and distant as ever.

As Alaric left, Althea returned from her grocery run, catching the tail end of the heated exchange. She watched silently as Emethy stormed back into the castle, her heart heavy with unresolved emotions.

Inside, Althea didn't ask any questions. She simply went to the kitchen and prepared a hot dark chocolate drink for Emethy. When she brought it to her, she handed over a blanket and said in a harsh, almost bitter tone, "Love is just an illusion."

Emethy took the drink, feeling the warmth seep into her hands but not into her heart. Althea's words resonated with her, deepening her sense of hurt. She agreed with Althea, feeling the sting of betrayal and the weight of her own unresolved emotions.

The following days were a blur of planning and preparation. Emethy's resolve to save Lyra only grew stronger. She continued to study the book, searching for the exact ritual she needed. The ingredients were rare and would take time to gather, but she was determined.

One evening, while Althea was out, Emethy took a deep breath and began to gather the necessary components. She moved quickly, her mind focused on the task at hand. She knew the risks, but she was willing to face them to free Lyra.

As Emethy worked, her thoughts drifted back to Alaric. Despite her anger, she couldn't shake the feeling that he genuinely cared. But the hurt and betrayal were too fresh. She couldn't afford to let her guard down again.

Late into the night, Emethy finally had everything she needed. She stood in her room, the book open before her, the ingredients laid out carefully. She took a deep breath, steeling herself for the ritual.

She began to chant the incantation softly, feeling the power of the words resonate within her. Her birthmark tingled, glowing faintly in the dim room. She closed her eyes, focusing her thoughts on Lyra, willing her voice to come through the elements.

"Emethy?" Lyra's voice was faint but clear, carried on the wind that rustled through the open window.

"Lyra, I can hear you!" Emethy's heart leaped with joy. "Where are you?"

"I'm still in the king's chamber," Lyra's voice echoed, now mingling with the sound of water dripping in the distance. "I was caught when I wandered into the biggest room of the council. There was a throne... I was curious, and I didn't know anyone could see me."

Emethy's relief at hearing Lyra's voice was mixed with guilt and determination. "I should have warned you to stay close. But we didn't know the king had the power to see spirits."

"It's not your fault," Lyra said gently. "We couldn't have known."

Emethy nodded, though Lyra couldn't see her. "I promise I'll get you out of there. We'll be together again soon."

Lyra's voice grew softer, almost a whisper. "Be careful, Emethy. The king's power is greater than we imagined."

"I will," Emethy vowed. "I won't let anything stop me."

As Lyra's voice faded, Emethy felt a renewed sense of determination. She knew the road ahead would be fraught with danger, but she was ready.

"In the dim light of her room, with shadows flickering around her, Emethy's resolve hardened. She knew the road ahead would be fraught with danger, but for Lyra, for herself, and for the truth that had been hidden for so long, she would face whatever came her way.

'I won't let anything stop me,' she vowed, her birthmark glowing faintly, a symbol of the power and determination that now burned within her."

Chapter 10

Market Encounters

&

New Friendship

Emethy's days at the Dim Light Castle had settled into a routine, punctuated by moments of tension and quiet determination. Althea, always the enigmatic figure, sensed the need for Emethy to venture outside the castle's walls and experience life beyond its shadows. One crisp morning, she handed Emethy a list of items needed from the village market.

"Take this," Althea said, her voice calm but insistent. "It will do you good to interact with the villagers. And we need these supplies."

Emethy accepted the list with a nod, though she felt a pang of reluctance. The market was bustling, filled with people, noise, and unfamiliar faces—an overwhelming contrast to the solitude of the castle. Nevertheless, she set off, determined to fulfil the task.

The village market was a vibrant place, alive with the shouts of vendors, the chatter of villagers, and the rich aromas of fresh produce and baked goods. Emethy wandered through the stalls, her eyes wide with curiosity and caution. She paused at a stand selling herbs and spices, unsure of how to approach the haggling process.

"Excuse me," a voice called out. Emethy turned to see a young man with tousled brown hair and bright blue eyes smiling at her. He wore simple, sturdy clothes, and his hands bore the marks of hard labor. "You look like you could use some help."

Emethy stiffened, her guard up. "I'm fine," she replied curtly, turning her attention back to the herbs.

The young man didn't take the hint. "I'm Kellan," he introduced himself. "My father's the village blacksmith. We make weapons for kings and warriors. You must be new here."

"Emethy," she replied reluctantly, not offering more.

Kellan grinned, undeterred by her cold demeanor. "Well, Emethy, if you need help bargaining, just let me know. I've been coming here since I could walk."

Despite herself, Emethy found his persistence oddly endearing. She relented, allowing him to guide her through the process of bargaining with the herb seller. Kellan's easy manner and genuine kindness began to chip away at her icy exterior.

"See? That wasn't so hard," Kellan said with a smile as they walked away with her purchase.

Emethy gave a small nod. "Thank you," she said, her tone softening slightly.

Days turned into weeks, and Emethy found herself returning to the market more frequently. Each time, she would encounter Kellan, who was always ready to assist and chat with her. Despite her initial resistance, she began to look forward to their interactions. Kellan's light-heartedness and unwavering friendliness were a stark contrast to the darkness she carried within her.

One afternoon, as they stood by a stall selling freshly baked bread, Kellan turned to her with a serious expression. "You know, Emethy, you don't have to keep pushing people away."

Emethy stiffened, her guard snapping back up. "I don't know what you're talking about."

Kellan sighed. "I've seen it in your eyes. You've been hurt, and you're afraid of losing people. But not everyone is going to leave you."

She looked away, her fingers tightening around the loaf of bread. "You don't understand."

"Maybe not," Kellan conceded. "But I'd like to. If you'll let me."

Emethy met his gaze, conflicted. For so long, she had built walls around her heart, protecting herself from the pain of loss. Yet, here was Kellan, persistent and genuine, offering her a glimpse of a different kind of connection.

As Emethy continued her visits to the market, she and Kellan grew closer. His unwavering kindness and patience began to thaw the icy barriers she had erected. He never pressed her for details about her past or her secrets, respecting her boundaries while subtly showing his support.

One evening, after a particularly long day at the market, Kellan walked Emethy back to the edge of the forest. The sun was setting, casting a warm golden glow over the landscape.

"Thank you for everything," Emethy said quietly, feeling a strange sense of gratitude and vulnerability.

Kellan smiled. "Anytime, Emethy. Remember, you don't have to face everything alone."

As she watched him walk away, Emethy couldn't help but feel a flicker of something she hadn't allowed herself to feel in a long time: hope.

Back at the Dim Light Castle, Emethy relayed her market experiences to Lyra, whose voice came through the rustling leaves and the gentle murmur of the river.

"Who is this Kellan?" Lyra asked, her tone light and curious.

"A village boy," Emethy replied, a hint of a smile in her voice. "He's been... helpful."

Lyra's laughter echoed softly. "It sounds like you've made a friend."

Emethy's smile faded slightly. "I don't know if I can trust him. I've lost so many people, Lyra. I don't want to lose anyone else."

"You won't lose me," Lyra said gently. "And maybe Kellan is someone you can trust too."

Emethy nodded, her resolve strengthening. She couldn't afford to be distracted by her emotions, not with the king still a threat and Lyra's fate hanging in the balance. But for now, she allowed herself to cherish the small moments of connection and kindness that Kellan had brought into her life.

One morning, as Emethy prepared to head to the market, Althea approached her. The older woman's eyes were thoughtful, her demeanor as enigmatic as ever.

"You seem different," Althea observed. "More at ease."

Emethy shrugged, trying to downplay the changes she felt within herself. "Just getting used to the village."

Althea nodded, a knowing smile playing on her lips. "Be careful, Emethy. The heart can be a powerful ally, but it can also be a dangerous vulnerability."

Emethy met her gaze, the words resonating deeply. "I'll be careful."

As she made her way to the market, Emethy couldn't shake the feeling that Althea knew more than she let on. The woman's cryptic wisdom always seemed to touch on truths that Emethy was still coming to understand.

At the market, Kellan greeted her with his usual cheerful demeanor. "Good to see you, Emethy. Ready for another day of bargaining?"

Emethy smiled, a genuine warmth in her expression. "Ready as I'll ever be."

As they moved through the bustling stalls, Emethy felt a growing sense of belonging. The villagers had come to recognize her, nodding in greeting or offering a kind word. Kellan's presence beside her was a comforting constant, his easy laughter and steady support a balm to her troubled spirit.

During one of their strolls, Kellan pointed out a small, hidden alcove behind the blacksmith's shop. "This is my favorite spot," he said, leading her to a bench nestled among blooming flowers. "Whenever I need to think or just get away, I come here."

Emethy sat beside him, the tranquility of the spot washing over her. "It's beautiful," she admitted, feeling a rare moment of peace.

Kellan's eyes sparkled with a mixture of hope and determination. "Emethy, I know you've been through a lot. But I want you to know that I'm here for you. Whatever you need, whenever you need it."

Emethy looked at him, her heart swelling with conflicting emotions. She wanted to believe in his sincerity, to trust in the possibility of friendship and maybe even something more. But the shadows of her past loomed large, reminding her of the pain of loss and betrayal.

That evening, as she returned to the Dim Light Castle, Emethystin couldn't shake the thoughts of Kellan from her mind. His kindness and persistence had touched her deeply, stirring emotions she had long buried.

Back in her room, she sat by the window, listening to the whispers of the wind and the gentle murmur of the river. Lyra's voice came through, comforting and familiar.

"Emethy, you deserve happiness," Lyra said softly. "Don't be afraid to let people in."

Emethy sighed, her heart heavy with uncertainty. "I don't want to lose anyone else, Lyra. I'm afraid."

"You're stronger than you think," Lyra replied. "And you're not alone. You have me, and you have Kellan."

Emethy nodded, feeling a surge of resolve. She couldn't let fear dictate her actions. She had faced demons, both literal and figurative, and she would face whatever came next with the same determination.

The days passed, and Emethy continued her visits to the market, her bond with Kellan growing stronger with each encounter. She began to confide in him, sharing bits and pieces of her past, her struggles, and her fears. Kellan listened with unwavering patience and understanding, never pressing her for more than she was willing to share.

One afternoon, as they sat in Kellan's favorite alcove, he turned to her with a serious expression. "Emethy, I need to tell you something."

Emethy's heart skipped a beat, her mind racing with possibilities. "What is it?"

Kellan took a deep breath, his eyes earnest. "I... I care about you, Emethy. More than just as a friend."

Emethy's breath caught in her throat, her heart pounding. She had sensed Kellan's feelings, but hearing them spoken aloud was both thrilling and terrifying.

"Kellan, I..." she began, struggling to find the right words. "I don't know if I'm ready for this."

Kellan nodded, his expression gentle. "I understand. I just wanted you to know how I feel. I don't expect anything from you, Emethy. I just want you to be happy."

Emethy felt her emotions a tumultuous mix of fear, gratitude, and something she hadn't allowed herself to feel in a long time: hope.

"Thank you," she whispered, her voice choked with emotion.

Kellan smiled, his eyes shining with sincerity. "Always, Emethy."

As Emethy made her way back to the Dim Light Castle, she felt a newfound sense of clarity and determination. She couldn't predict the future or shield herself from all pain, but she could choose to embrace the connections and support that surrounded her.

Back in her room, she listened to Lyra's voice, carried by the wind and water, feeling a sense of unity and strength.

"We're in this together, Lyra," she said softly. "No matter what happens."

Lyra's voice echoed with warmth and reassurance. "Always, Emethy."

With renewed resolve, Emethystin knew she would face whatever challenges lay ahead, supported by those who cared for her. Together, they would uncover the truth, confront the darkness, and forge a path towards a brighter future.

Chapter 11

The Strike of Allies

&

Revelations

The forest was serene that day, its tranquility a stark contrast to the turmoil that would soon envelop Emethy's world. She had left the castle early with the goal of gathering rare herbs essential for Althea's mysterious potions. The crisp winter air bit at her cheeks as she trudged through the snow, her boots crunching on the frosty ground. Emethy moved silently through the dense forest, the moonlight filtering through the canopy above, casting an ethereal glow on the path ahead. As she reached a clearing, a chilling sensation ran down her spine. She halted, her senses heightened. There, at the edge of the shadows, she saw it—a dark, amorphous figure, its form barely distinguishable from the night itself. The black shadow seemed to pulse with a malevolent energy, its presence suffocating the very air around it. Emethy's heart raced, her hand instinctively reaching for her dagger. The shadow didn't move, but its mere existence was a threat, a sinister omen that something far more dangerous lurked in the depths of the forest.

Emethy's mind wandered back to Seraphina and the danger that seemed to loom ever closer.

Back at the castle, Althea stayed behind, her silhouette flickering in the dim candlelight of the castle's study. The old, weathered tomes spread out before her, their ancient pages whispering secrets of forgotten magic. Althea's fingers traced the intricate symbols, her mind focused on the research that might hold the key to their survival.

Meanwhile, Seraphina was alone in another part of the castle. She had been tidying up, humming softly to herself, the black cat curling around her ankles as if sensing something amiss. The tranquillity was shattered by the sudden sound of heavy boots and the crash of a door being forced open. The King's Guards, his most loyal and ruthless Guards, stormed in, their presence a dark omen.

Seraphina's heart pounded as she faced them. "What do you want?" she demanded, her voice steady despite her fear.

"We know someone helped you escape the King's captivity," the leader of the group snarled. "Where are they?"

Seraphina's eyes flashed with defiance. "I don't know what you're talking about."

The Guards ransacked the room, their search brutal and thorough. They found nothing incriminating, but it didn't matter. They had their orders. Seraphina fought bravely as they dragged her out, her screams echoing through the empty halls.

Hours later, Emethy returned, the weight of her gathered herbs feeling insignificant compared to the dread that gnawed at her stomach. As she approached the castle, Emethy felt a chill that had nothing to do with the winter air. She rushed inside, her heart sinking as she saw the state of Seraphina's room. Furniture was overturned, belongings scattered, a testament to the violence that had occurred.

"Seraphina!" Emethy called, her voice breaking with desperation. There was no answer, only the oppressive silence.

Althea appeared in the doorway, her brow furrowed with confusion and concern. "What happened here?" she asked, her voice uncharacteristically soft.

Emethy's fists clenched in fury. "It was the King. His Guards took Seraphina."

Althea's eyes widened in shock. "Why? What does he want with her?"

Emethy's mind raced. She couldn't reveal everything about Seraphina's escape from the King's captivity or the rituals she had been studying. Althea didn't know about the deeper intricacies of their struggles, the magic, the danger.

"He must have found out she escaped," Emethy said, trying to keep her voice steady. "He's looking for whoever helped her."

Althea's face hardened. "Do you know who might have done this?"

Emethy met her gaze, her own eyes filled with determination. "It doesn't matter now. We need to get Seraphina back. I can't let him keep her."

Althea placed a comforting hand on Emethy's shoulder. "We will get her back, Emethy. But we need a plan. Rushing in without thinking will only get us all killed."

Emethy nodded, swallowing her rage. "You're right. We need to be smart about this. But first, we need to find out where they took her."

Althea's eyes were thoughtful. "I might know someone who can help. An old contact of mine in the nearby village. They might have information on the King's movements."

Emethy's resolve hardened. "Then I'll go tonight. We can't waste any time."

As Emethy prepared to leave, Althea stayed behind, her presence a comforting anchor in the darkened castle. Emethy felt the weight of responsibility settle on her shoulders. She couldn't afford to fail. The King's actions had ignited a fire within her, a determination that burned hotter than ever. She would rescue Seraphina, no matter the cost.

Night fell, and the forest became a dark, shadowy maze. Emethy moved swiftly and silently, her senses heightened. She reached the village under the cover of darkness, slipping into the narrow alleys and seeking out Althea's contact.

She found him in a dimly lit tavern, a grizzled old man with eyes that seemed to see everything. Emethy spoke to him in hushed tones, and he nodded, his expression grave.

"I've heard rumors," he said, his voice a raspy whisper. "The King's Guards took someone to the old fortress near the eastern cliffs. It's heavily guarded."

Emethy's heart pounded. "Thank you," she said, her voice filled with gratitude and urgency.

As she made her way back to the castle, Emethy's mind was a whirlwind of thoughts and plans. She knew the fortress he spoke of, and she knew it wouldn't be easy. But Seraphina was worth the risk.

Back at the castle, Althea was deep in her research, the dim light casting long shadows across the room. The tension was palpable as she awaited Emethy's return. The castle, usually a place of relative safety, now felt like a cage of impending doom.

Emethy arrived breathless, her urgency evident. "I found out where they took her," she said, her voice low but resolute. "The old fortress near the eastern cliffs."

Althea nodded, her expression grim. "We need allies," she said. "We can't do this alone."

Emethy nodded, her resolve unwavering. "We'll find them. We'll do whatever it takes to bring her back."

The night air was cold, but Emethy felt a burning fire within her. The King's Guards had made a grave mistake. They had taken someone she cared about, and she would stop at nothing to rescue Seraphina and bring the King to justice. As the first light of dawn began to break, Emethy and Althea stood together, their minds set on the challenges ahead. The road would be perilous, but they were ready to face it together.

The castle was quiet as they prepared for their mission. Emethy and Althea gathered their supplies, ensuring they had everything they needed for the rescue. Emethy packed her sword, her bow and arrows, and a small pouch of healing herbs. Althea brought her potions, each one labeled with intricate symbols that Emethy couldn't decipher.

"We should rest," Althea advised. "We need to be at our best tomorrow."

Emethy nodded, though she knew sleep would be hard to come by. Her thoughts were consumed with worry for Seraphina and the challenges they would face. She lay in bed, staring at the ceiling, willing herself to relax. Finally, exhaustion overtook her, and she drifted into a fitful sleep.

Emethy was resolute in her decision to rescue Seraphina. She knew she couldn't undertake this perilous mission alone. The urgency of the situation left no room for hesitation. Her first call was to Kellan, whose unwavering support and expertise with weapons made him a crucial ally. His arrival at the dimly lit castle was swift and decisive.

"Seraphina needs us," Emethy said, her voice edged with determination as she briefed Kellan. "The King has no knowledge of me yet, but he's aware someone assisted Seraphina in escaping. Althea will stay behind to safeguard the castle, but she's sending her cat with us. We need to move quickly."

Kellan's eyes met hers with a mixture of resolve and concern. "Count me in. We'll get Seraphina out, no matter the cost."

Emethy also enlisted the help of Rian, an agile and skilled fighter who had trained under Althea. With Kellan and Rian by her side, and Althea's black cat leading the way, they embarked on their journey to the kingdom. The air was thick with anticipation as they travelled, the shadows of the dimly lit landscape passing by.

The journey was arduous, but Emethy felt a strange comfort in the whispers of the wind. It seemed to guide her, offering encouragement as they drew closer to their destination. The wind carried faint murmurs of hope, strengthening her resolve to see the mission through.

Upon reaching the outskirts of the kingdom, Emethy guided her companions to the hidden entrance Prince Alaric had previously shown her. The passage was concealed behind an overgrown thicket and was known only to a few. They slipped through the narrow opening, emerging into the heart of the enemy's stronghold.

The castle's interior was a maze of corridors and stairways, each shadowed with foreboding. Emethy led the way with practiced stealth, her senses finely attuned to the slightest sound. Every creak of the floorboards and distant murmur of voices heightened their tension.

Their search led them to the chamber where Lyra's spirit was imprisoned. The room was dark and oppressive, with heavy iron bars and arcane symbols etched into the stone walls. Emethy drew a deep breath and began the ritual she had painstakingly learned. Her voice wove through the incantations with a mix of confidence and trepidation.

The atmosphere in the chamber shifted as magical energy swirled around them. Lyra's spirit began to materialize, her form slowly coalescing into a visible, radiant presence.

"Lyra, you're free now," Emethy said softly, her eyes brimming with relief.

Lyra's spirit, now fully formed and glowing with an otherworldly light, smiled gratefully. "Thank you, Emethy. I knew you would come for me."

There was no time for celebration, however. The urgency of their mission drove Emethy to find Seraphina. She led the way through the castle, her heart racing as they navigated the labyrinthine corridors.

They finally reached the cell where Seraphina was being held. The sight of her, weak and battered, filled Emethy with a surge of protective fury. She quickly unlocked the cell, and they began to move Seraphina to safety.

But their escape was cut short by the sudden appearance of the King's Guards. The Guards, dark and menacing, attacked with a ruthless efficiency. A fierce battle erupted. Kellan and Rian fought valiantly, their skills complementing Emethy's as they struggled to hold back the Guards.

Amid the chaos, Seraphina was injured. She fell to the ground, her breaths shallow and ragged. Emethy's heart sank as she knelt beside her, trying to stem the flow of blood from her wounds.

"Seraphina, stay with us!" Emethy pleaded, her voice choked with emotion.

Seraphina's eyes, though dim with pain, held a spark of urgency. "Emethy… I don't have much time left."

"What is it? Tell me what I need to know!" Emethy urged, her hands trembling.

Seraphina's voice was barely a whisper. "The scripture… it speaks of someone born from darkness, wielding a sword… and their path to free the souls, to rule the spirit world. You must find this person. They are the key to freeing the trapped souls in this kingdom."

Emethy's mind raced with the weight of Seraphina's words. "Who is this person? How do I find them?"

Seraphina's gaze was intense, her voice growing fainter. "Look for the one who bears both the mark of darkness and light. They will guide you."

With a final, shuddering breath, Seraphina's life ebbed away, leaving Emethy with a profound sense of loss and urgency. She gathered Seraphina's body, her heart heavy with grief, and turned to Kellan and Rian.

"We need to leave," Emethy said, her voice firm despite the tears streaming down her face. "We need to find this person—whoever they are. They hold the key to freeing the souls and overthrowing the King."

They retraced their steps through the hidden passage, their escape fraught with tension and danger. As they emerged into the night, Emethy could feel the gravity of her mission pressing down upon her. The King's cruelty was far more extensive than she had imagined, and the task ahead was daunting.

Yet, with Lyra's spirit now at her side, Kellan's unwavering support, and Rian's skilled assistance, Emethy felt a flicker of hope amidst the darkness. They were bound by a shared purpose, and together, they would face the challenges that lay ahead.

As they journeyed away from the kingdom, the wind seemed to whisper encouragement once more, guiding them towards their next destination. Emethy knew that the path ahead was fraught with peril, but the fire of determination burned brightly within her. She was ready to confront whatever came next and to fulfil the quest that Seraphina had entrusted to her.

Chapter 12

A Friend's Warning

The evening sky was painted with shades of deep blue and purple as Emethy, Kellan, and Rian journeyed away from the kingdom. The solemnity of their mission weighed heavily on their hearts. They had left the castle far behind, their destination a secluded riverside where they planned to lay Seraphina to rest with the reverence she deserved. The tranquil gurgle of the river offered a stark contrast to the grief that enveloped them.

The trio arrived at the river's edge as the sun dipped below the horizon, leaving a soft twilight glow. The area was serene, surrounded by tall trees that whispered in the evening breeze. Emethy and Kellan began preparing for the burial, setting out the items needed for the ritual. Rian stood by, his face a mix of sadness and contemplation, as he watched the somber preparations.

The ritual was one of ancient tradition, meant to honor the deceased and guide their spirit to the next realm. Emethy moved with practiced grace, her voice steady despite the emotions that threatened to overwhelm her. She chanted softly, her words a bridge between the physical world and the spirit realm. Kellan and Rian assisted with the ritual, their movements respectful and deliberate.

As the final incantations were spoken and the ritual concluded, the night settled into darkness, broken only by the flickering light of the candles they had used. The burial was complete, and the sense of loss hung heavily in the air. Emethy felt a pang of sadness but also a deep resolve to continue their mission.

"Thank you," Emethy said quietly to Kellan and Rian, her voice tinged with exhaustion. "We need to keep moving, but for now, I'm grateful for your support."

Rian nodded, his gaze lingering on Emethy. There was something in his eyes—an emotion he couldn't quite name, but it was clear that his feelings for Emethy were evolving into something deeper. He had always admired her strength and determination, but now he found himself drawn to her in a way that went beyond mere respect.

As the night progressed, the trio set up a temporary camp by the river. The crackling fire provided some warmth against the encroaching chill, and they tried to rest, though the tension from their recent ordeal made sleep elusive.

A sudden, bone-chilling sound shattered the quiet night—a low, guttural growl that seemed to emanate from the very ground beneath them. Emethy, already on edge from the day's events, jolted upright, her senses on high alert. Kellan and Rian followed suit, their expressions shifting to one of concern.

"What was that?" Rian asked, his voice barely above a whisper.

"I don't know," Emethy replied, her eyes scanning the darkened forest. "But we need to be prepared."

The growl intensified, morphing into a roar that reverberated through the trees. The underbrush around their camp began to rustle violently, and before they could react, a massive, shadowy figure emerged from the darkness. It was a creature of nightmarish proportions, with glowing eyes and a hulking, grotesque form that seemed to writhe with malevolent intent.

"It's a demon!" Kellan shouted, drawing his sword with a steady hand despite his pale face. "Everyone, get ready!"

The demon let out a deafening roar and lunged towards them, its massive claws slashing through the air with terrifying speed. The battle was immediate and brutal. Kellan and Rian fought valiantly, their blades flashing in the dim light of the fire. Emethy, despite her exhaustion and the fresh grief from Seraphina's burial, joined the fray with grim determination.

The demon was formidable, its attacks swift and merciless. Emethy fought fiercely but found herself overwhelmed by the creature's power. The demon's claws struck her shoulder, sending her sprawling to the ground. Pain shot through her body, but she forced herself to stay conscious.

"Emethy!" Kellan's voice broke through the chaos, his face etched with panic as he tried to fend off the demon's blows.

Amidst the turmoil, Lyra's spectral voice echoed through the night, her tone filled with distress. "Emethy! Please be careful! You're hurt badly!"

Emethy's vision blurred with pain, but she could see Lyra's ghostly form hovering nearby, shimmering with concern. Despite the agony, Emethy managed to focus on Lyra's voice. "Lyra… stay calm. I'm still fighting."

The battle raged on, and it became evident that they were losing ground. The demon's relentless attacks and the relentless rain made it impossible to gain the upper hand. Kellan and Rian fought desperately to protect Emethy, but their strength was waning.

"We need to retreat!" Kellan shouted over the din of the battle. "We can't defeat it here!"

Emethy, barely able to stand, nodded in agreement. The group quickly gathered their belongings and prepared to flee. Rian helped Emethy, his face pale with worry, while Kellan kept a vigilant watch on the demon's movements.

As they fled through the rain-soaked forest, the demon's roar echoed behind them, a haunting reminder of the danger they had narrowly escaped. The rain mingled with Emethy's blood, making the forest seem even darker and more oppressive. Lyra's voice was a small comfort amidst the chaos, her presence a soothing balm for Emethy's frayed nerves.

"Hold on, Emethy," Lyra urged, her voice trembling. "We'll find a way through this. You're stronger than you know."

Despite the pain and exhaustion, Emethy felt a surge of determination. The demon had driven them away, but it hadn't defeated them. They would find another way, another path to continue their mission.

They finally reached a small, hidden cave, offering them a brief respite from the storm and the dangers of the night. The cave was dark and damp but provided a much-needed sanctuary. As they settled in, Emethy's mind drifted to the prophecy Seraphina had spoken of and the person born from darkness and light. She knew that finding this individual was crucial, and that their journey was far from over.

Inside the cave, Kellan and Rian worked quickly to tend to Emethy's injuries. Kellan expertly bandaged her wound, his hands steady despite the fear in his eyes. Rian fetched water and medicinal herbs, his face etched with concern.

Emethy winced as Kellan worked on her shoulder. "Thank you," she said through gritted teeth. "We need to keep moving, but we have to make sure I'm fit to travel."

"We'll stay here until you're better," Kellan replied firmly. "But we can't afford to rest too long. The King's Guards are still out there."

Emethy nodded, her gaze distant. "I know. We need to find the person from the prophecy. We need to free the souls and end the King's reign."

As they made a fire to warm themselves, Lyra's voice continued to offer reassurance, even though she could only be seen by Emethy. "Emethy, you're not alone. We'll find a way."

Emethy looked at the spectral figure, a flicker of hope in her eyes. "Thank you, Lyra. Your presence is a comfort."

The night wore on, and the storm outside showed no sign of letting up. The cave was a sanctuary of sorts but also served as a reminder of the challenges they faced. Emethy's strength gradually returned, fuelled by the unwavering support of her friends and the promise of the journey that lay ahead.

As dawn approached, the rain began to ease, leaving a misty haze over the forest. The fire crackled softly, casting warm light on the cave's walls. Emethy took a deep breath and stood, her resolve strengthened by the trials she had faced.

"We'll head back out soon," Emethy said, her voice firm despite her exhaustion. "We need to find the person from the prophecy and free the souls trapped by the King."

Kellan and Rian exchanged determined glances, their resolve matching Emethy's. "We're with you," Kellan said. "Whatever it takes."

Rian's gaze lingered on Emethy, his feelings for her evident. "We'll get through this together," he said, his voice filled with quiet determination.

The group prepared to leave the safety of the cave, their spirits lifted by the fire's warmth and the promise of a new day. The path ahead was fraught with danger, but Emethy knew that they had the strength and resolve to see it through. The echoes of the night, though daunting, had only strengthened her determination. They were not just fighting for their survival but for the freedom and justice that Seraphina had sought to achieve.

With renewed purpose, Emethy, Kellan, and Rian stepped out into the misty morning, ready to face whatever challenges lay ahead. The journey would be long and arduous, but their resolve was unwavering. The fate of the kingdom—and the souls within it—depended on their success.

Emethy's wounds ached with every step as the trio made their way to the small, ramshackle house on the edge of a remote village. The air was thick with the scent of damp earth and decay, a fitting backdrop for the dilapidated abode of the local butcher. With her strength waning, Emethy welcomed the prospect of rest despite the uneasy feeling the butcher's predatory gaze invoked.

The butcher, a burly man with eyes that gleamed with unspoken malice, welcomed them with a curt nod. "You can rest here," he said gruffly, pointing to a small, shadowy room at the back of the house. His eyes lingered a moment too long on Emethy, making her skin crawl. "Make yourselves comfortable."

Kellan and Rian exchanged wary glances but helped Emethy into the room. It was a dreary, cramped space, furnished only with a sagging bed and a wooden chair. The cat, Emethy's ever-present companion, slinked under the bed and settled there with a watchful gaze.

"Thank you," Emethy murmured, her voice barely audible. She sank onto the bed, her exhaustion overpowering her.

"Rest now," Kellan said softly. "We'll be back soon."

As the day passed, the sounds of the village outside faded into a rhythmic lullaby. Kellan and Rian ventured out to gather supplies and fetch water, leaving Emethy alone with the sinister butcher.

The butcher, sensing the absence of Kellan and Rian, approached Emethy with a smirk. He sauntered into the room where she lay, his gaze roving over her with an unsettling hunger.

"You should be more careful," he said, his voice dripping with condescension. "Out here, people can be less... friendly."

Emethy, feeling his gaze like a physical weight, ignored him and retreated back to the bed, pulling the thin blanket up over her shoulders. The cat, observing the butcher's approach, hissed furiously, its eyes glowing with an unearthly light.

The butcher, unmoved by the cat's warnings, chuckled darkly and left the room. Lyra, the spirit who had taken a quiet vigil over Emethy, watched from a shadowed corner. Disturbed by the butcher's presence and his intentions, Lyra's form flickered and grew darker, a spectral storm brewing around her.

As night fell, the full moon rose high in the sky, its light casting an eerie glow through the window. Emethy lay on the bed, her breathing shallow and steady as the moonlight illuminated her birthmark, causing it to glow with an otherworldly radiance.

In the dead of night, when silence had settled like a shroud over the house, the butcher crept back to Emethy's room. He slipped through the door with practiced ease, his movements silent and menacing. His eyes gleamed with cruel intent as he approached the bed where Emethy lay, her face illuminated by the ghostly moonlight.

The cat, ever vigilant, watched with a low, rumbling growl. The room was filled with a palpable sense of dread. As the butcher reached out to touch her, a sudden, sharp hiss filled the air. The cat's eyes blazed with an intense light, but the butcher was too focused on Emethy to pay it any heed.

Emethy stirred, her eyes snapping open to find the butcher looming over her. A surge of panic mixed with anger rose within her. "What are you doing?" she shouted, her voice breaking through the silence.

The butcher's sneer widened. "Just making sure you're safe, darling," he said, his hand inching closer.

"No! Get away from me!" Emethy screamed. The full moon's light seemed to intensify, and her birthmark glowed brighter than ever. Without understanding how or why, she felt an overwhelming force surge through her. The room seemed to vibrate with energy.

The butcher's expression changed from amusement to shock as an invisible, crushing force twisted his body in unnatural ways. He tried to scream, but no sound came out as he collapsed, his body contorted and lifeless. The power of Emethy's birthmark had acted on its own, driven by her primal fear and anger.

Kellan and Rian, who had just returned to the house, rushed into the room, alarmed by Emethy's screams. They froze at the doorway, their eyes widening in horror at the sight of the butcher's twisted corpse.

"What happened?" Kellan demanded, his voice urgent.

"I... I don't know," Emethy stammered, her face pale. "He was trying to... and then... I don't know how I did that."

Rian's eyes were troubled as he looked at the butcher's body. "This was our only place for the night," he said, frustration seeping into his voice. "What are we going to do now?"

"We need to leave," Kellan said, trying to keep calm. "We can't stay here."

The next day, with heavy hearts and a grim sense of duty, they buried the butcher in a shallow grave near the house. The sun was a harsh contrast to the night's horrors, casting long shadows over the grave as they worked in silence.

As they walked away from the burial site, Emethy's thoughts were consumed by confusion and fear. The power she had unleashed, the glowing birthmark, and the butcher's death weighed heavily on her mind. She had acted instinctively, but the true nature of her powers remained a mystery.

Kellan placed a reassuring hand on her shoulder. "We'll figure it out, Emethy," he said softly. "Whatever this is, we'll figure it out together."

Emethy nodded, though her mind was still reeling. Her newfound ability was both terrifying and confusing, and she felt a growing sense of responsibility to understand it. With Kellan and Rian by her side, she knew they would face whatever challenges lay ahead.

As they continued their journey, Emethy couldn't shake the memory of the butcher's lifeless body and the strange, otherworldly power she had felt. She knew that understanding her hidden strength was crucial to their quest, and she was determined to uncover the truth behind her abilities. But for now, all she could do was press forward, one step at a time, with the support of her companions and the weight of her newfound power on her shoulders.

Chapter 13

The Storm Within

&

Silent Wounds

The corridors of Dim Light Castle were silent in the dead of night, save for the occasional creak of ancient wood and the soft whisper of the wind outside. Althea, ever vigilant, was making her rounds through the castle, her footsteps echoing softly in the empty halls. Her duties as the protector of the castle extended beyond mere strategy and leadership; she took it upon herself to ensure the well-being of those within its walls, especially now with Emethy recovering from her injuries.

As Althea passed by Emethy's room, she heard a faint, distressed murmur coming from within. The sound was soft but insistent, carried on the night air. Pausing,

Althea's keen senses picked up on the urgency and discomfort in the murmurs. She moved closer, her hand resting on the door handle.

The door creaked open slowly, and Althea slipped inside, careful not to make any noise. The room was dimly lit by the moonlight streaming through the window, casting long, ethereal shadows across the floor. Emethy lay in bed, tangled in the sheets, her brow glistening with sweat. Her breathing was uneven, and her murmurs were punctuated by occasional whimpers of distress.

Althea approached the bed, her eyes narrowing in concern. She could see that Emethy was deeply troubled, her sleep disturbed by something that seemed more than mere dreams. Despite the temptation to wake her and offer comfort, Althea chose to observe silently, respecting the boundaries of Emethy's privacy.

As she watched, it became clear to Althea that Emethy's fear wasn't rooted in the grandiose threats they had faced—monsters, enemies, and the dark forces they battled. Instead, the terror that twisted Emethy's face in her sleep seemed to be rooted in something much smaller, something intimate and personal. It was as if the enormity of the world outside was less daunting to her than the subtle, insidious fears that lurked within.

Althea lingered for a while, noting the patterns of Emethy's distress. She was clearly a young woman grappling with internal struggles that were overshadowed by her more immediate fears. Eventually, Althea stepped back, allowing Emethy to continue her troubled sleep. She closed the door softly behind her and made her way back to her quarters, her mind racing with thoughts about the young woman under her care.

The next morning, as the first light of dawn began to filter through the castle windows, Althea found Emethy already awake and sitting by the window, her gaze distant and contemplative. The room was filled with the soft, healing aroma of herbs, a reminder of the previous day's care.

Althea entered the room, her demeanor as composed as ever, though there was a trace of concern in her eyes. "Good morning, Emethy," she said, her voice carrying a tone of quiet authority. "I hope you slept well."

Emethy turned to face her, attempting to mask the lingering exhaustion and distress from the night before.

"Good morning," she replied, her voice subdued. "I'm feeling better, thank you."

Althea studied her for a moment before speaking again. "Last night, I heard you murmuring in your sleep. It sounded as though you were quite troubled. Is there something you'd like to talk about? Sometimes, speaking about our fears can help us find clarity."

Emethy's face tightened, a flicker of discomfort crossing her features. She had expected Althea to notice her distress, but she hadn't anticipated this direct approach. She shook her head, her gaze dropping to the floor. "It was nothing," she said, her voice steady but resolute. "Just a bad dream."

Althea's eyes were sharp and perceptive, but she did not press the issue further. She could see that Emethy was not ready to open up, and she respected that boundary. "Very well," Althea said, her tone softening slightly. "If you ever feel ready to talk, know that I'm here to listen. Sometimes, even the smallest fears can be the hardest to face alone."

Emethy nodded, her expression unreadable. "Thank you," she said quietly. "I appreciate your understanding."

Althea gave a nod of acknowledgment and turned to leave the room. "I'll be around if you need anything. Take care."

As Althea walked out of the room, she couldn't shake the feeling that there was more to Emethy's fears than met the eye. The young woman was strong and resilient, but her internal struggles were clearly significant. Althea resolved to keep a close watch on Emethy, offering support without intrusion.

Emethy watched Althea leave, her mind already turning over the events of the previous night. She had hoped to keep her fears buried deep, but the reality of her situation was catching up with her. The nightmares and the sense of vulnerability were becoming more pressing, and she knew she needed to confront these fears sooner or later.

For now, she chose to focus on her recovery and the tasks at hand. The challenges they faced were not just external; they were internal as well. As she continued to heal and regain her strength, Emethy knew she would have to confront her own demons—both those within and those lurking in the shadows of her past.

One bright morning, the castle was quiet except for the clattering of utensils in the kitchen. Ploma and Emethy were preparing a meal, their movements coordinated in a familiar rhythm. Althea had gone out for personal affairs, leaving the two young women to manage the day's chores.

Ploma hummed a soft tune as she chopped vegetables, her face lit up with a serene smile. Emethy, on the other hand, was quieter, focused on kneading dough, her thoughts distant. Lyra floated nearby, her ethereal presence only visible to Emethy, watching the interaction with a curious eye.

As they worked, Ploma suddenly broke the silence, her voice light and airy. "You know, Emethy, I've known Kellan since we were children. He's always been so kind and brave. I've had a soft spot for him for as long as I can remember."

Emethy's hands stilled for a moment, but she quickly resumed her task, her expression unreadable. Lyra's eyes flicked to Emethy, sensing the tension.

Ploma continued, seemingly oblivious to the change in atmosphere. "Kellan's always been there for me, through thick and thin. I suppose it's only natural to develop feelings for someone like that."

Emethy nodded slightly, her lips pressed into a thin line. "I see," she said quietly, not trusting herself to say more.

Ploma, lost in her memories, didn't notice Emethy's lack of enthusiasm. She kept talking, her words a stream of affection and admiration for Kellan. Emethy's grip on the dough tightened, her knuckles whitening. After a few more moments of listening to Ploma's prattle, she couldn't take it anymore.

"I need to fetch some water," Emethy said abruptly, wiping her hands on a cloth. "Excuse me."

Without waiting for a response, she turned and left the kitchen, her footsteps echoing in the empty corridor. Ploma watched her go, a look of confusion and hurt crossing her face.

Outside, Emethy walked briskly to the well, her mind a whirlwind of emotions. She felt an odd mix of anger, sadness, and frustration. She had kept her feelings for Kellan hidden, and hearing Ploma speak so openly about him had stirred something inside her.

"Why did I have to listen to that?" she muttered to herself, pulling up the bucket of water. "Why did it have to be her?"

Lyra appeared beside her, her ghostly form shimmering in the daylight. "Emethy, you don't have to hide your feelings. It's okay to be upset."

Emethy shook her head, blinking back tears. "I can't, Lyra. I can't let myself be vulnerable. Not now. Not with everything that's happening."

She took a deep breath, trying to compose herself. "I just need to focus on what's important. Kellan deserves to be happy, even if it's not with me."

As she turned to head back to the castle, she saw Althea approaching. The older woman's stern face softened slightly when she saw Emethy.

"Are you alright?" Althea asked, her eyes narrowing in concern.

Emethy forced a smile. "I'm fine. Just needed some air."

Althea studied her for a moment, then nodded. "Alright. Let's head back. We've got a lot to do."

They returned to the castle, where Ploma was still in the kitchen, her expression troubled. Emethy felt a pang of guilt for her earlier rudeness but didn't know how to bridge the gap.

Althea sensed the tension and decided not to pry. She knew Emethy well enough to understand that pushing her would only make things worse. Instead, she focused on the task at hand, guiding the girls through the rest of the meal preparation.

Throughout the day, Emethy remained distant, her thoughts preoccupied. She knew she needed to address her feelings, both for Kellan and her reaction to Ploma's confession, but the wounds were still too fresh. As the sun set and the castle grew quiet again, Emethy found herself staring out the window, wondering if she would ever find the strength to confront her emotions and the complex web of relationships that bound them all together.

The next few days passed in a similar fashion, with Emethy throwing herself into her work, trying to avoid any deeper conversations. Ploma, sensing the undercurrent of tension, tried to give Emethy space while still offering her support.

One evening, as they sat around the dinner table, Kellan noticed the strained silence. He glanced between Emethy and Ploma, his brow furrowing in concern. "Is everything alright?"

Emethy forced a smile, nodding. "Just tired. It's been a long day."

Ploma gave a hesitant smile as well. "Yes, everything's fine."

Kellan didn't seem convinced but decided not to press further. He turned the conversation to lighter topics, hoping to ease the tension.

As the days turned into weeks, Emethy continued to grapple with her feelings. She knew she couldn't avoid the issue forever, but for now, she focused on her recovery and the tasks at hand. With Lyra's quiet support and the unspoken understanding between her and Ploma, she found a way to keep moving forward, even if the path ahead remained uncertain and fraught with emotional challenges.

That night, Althea sat on the edge of Emethy's bed, her eyes filled with concern. Emethy lay propped up against pillows, her face pale but determined.

"Emethy," Althea began gently, "is it taking too long for you to recover? You're a healer, yet your wounds seem to linger. Is there something more we should be concerned about?"

Emethy sighed, avoiding Althea's gaze. "I don't know, Althea. I've done everything I can, but it feels like something is blocking my healing. I don't understand it myself."

Althea studied her for a moment, sensing there was more Emethy wasn't sharing. "We need you at your full strength, Emethy. If there's anything you're holding back, you must tell me."

Emethy looked away, her voice barely above a whisper. "I'll try to figure it out."

The next day, Althea called everyone to gather for dinner. The atmosphere was tense, an unspoken worry hanging over them all. As they settled around the table, the conversation started light but soon took a darker turn.

During the meal, Rian and Kellen's usual banter escalated. "You're being reckless," Rian snapped, his eyes flashing with anger. "We can't afford any more mistakes."

Kellen's temper flared. "And what exactly are you implying?"

Rian's voice grew louder, more heated. "It's Emethy's fault we're in this mess. She killed a man without any serious reason!"

The room fell silent, all eyes turning to Emethy. Ploma and Althea looked stunned, unaware of the incident with the butcher.

Emethy's face turned pale, a mix of shame and anger flashing across her features. Without a word, she stood up and walked out of the castle, her steps hurried and unsteady. The cat, sensing her distress, followed closely behind.

"Emethy, wait!" Ploma called after her, but Althea placed a hand on her shoulder.

"Let her be," Althea said quietly. "She needs space."

Emethy's footsteps echoed in the stillness as she made her way into the forest. The familiar sights and sounds offered little comfort as her mind raced with Rian's accusations and the memories of that night. The cat stayed close, its presence a silent comfort.

She reached a clearing and sank to the ground, tears streaming down her face. The full moon hung above, casting a soft glow over the trees. Emethy's birthmark began to glow faintly, a reminder of the power she still didn't fully understand.

As she sat there, the cat curled up beside her, purring softly. Emethy stroked its fur, finding some solace in the simple act. The forest seemed to whisper around her, the rustling leaves and distant calls of nocturnal creatures a soothing lullaby.

Back at the castle, the tension lingered. Althea and Ploma exchanged worried glances, both knowing they needed to address the underlying issues that had been brought to light. Kellen stared at his plate, guilt and frustration warring within him.

"We can't let this divide us," Althea said firmly. "Emethy needs our support now more than ever. We need to find a way to help her, and ourselves."

Ploma nodded, her eyes filled with determination. "We will. We'll get through this together."

The night wore on, and Emethy remained in the forest, her thoughts slowly settling. She knew she couldn't run from her problems forever. Tomorrow, she would return to the castle and face whatever awaited her. But for now, she let the tranquility of the forest wash over her, finding a brief respite from the turmoil within.

As dawn broke, Emethy rose from her spot, determination hardening her resolve. She walked back towards the castle, the cat at her heels. She had to face her friends, her fears, and the unknown power within her. With each step, she felt a bit stronger, ready to confront whatever came next.

Chapter 14

Healing & Haunting Truth

As the sun began its slow descent, casting long shadows across the forest, Althea decided it was time to find Emethy. The argument at dinner still weighed heavily on her mind, and she couldn't shake the worry she felt for Emethy. Gathering her resolve, she headed into the forest, following the faint trail left by her troubled friend.

Emethy sat in the clearing, staring blankly at the sky. She heard the crunch of leaves and looked up to see Althea approaching. Her expression softened, and she offered a weak smile.

"Althea," she greeted quietly.

Althea sat beside her, the silence stretching between them. "Emethy, I'm here if you want to talk. About anything."

For a moment, Emethy hesitated. The memories of the butcher's incident, Rian's accusations, and her own confusion swirled in her mind. But something about Althea's presence, her unwavering support, made Emethy feel safe.

With a deep breath, Emethy began. "That night at the butcher's house... it was the full moon. My birthmark was glowing, and I was exhausted. I didn't realize the power I had... not until it was too late."

Althea listened intently, her eyes never leaving Emethy's face. "Tell me what happened."

Emethy recounted the events, her voice trembling. "The butcher had bad intentions. I could feel it. When he tried to touch me, something inside me snapped. I didn't mean to... I didn't know I could do that. It just happened."

Althea nodded, understanding the gravity of Emethy's words. "Rian doesn't know what you've been through, Emethy. He can't understand the fear and power you felt in that moment."

Emethy's eyes filled with tears. "He thinks I killed an innocent man out of anger. But I was scared, Althea. I didn't mean to hurt anyone."

Althea placed a comforting hand on Emethy's shoulder. "Individuals may not always comprehend one another unless they have shared a similar experience. Some people are extremely sensitive to suffering; they are known as empaths. Some, nevertheless, are unable to. It's crucial that you comprehend who you are."

Emethy looked at Althea, her expression searching. "But what if I don't understand myself?"

"That's a journey we all take, Emethy. And it's not an easy one. But you're strong, and you have people who care about you. We'll figure this out together."

Emethy wiped away her tears, a small smile breaking through. "Thank you, Althea. For listening, and for being here."

Althea smiled back, a rare warmth in her eyes. "I'm glad you opened up. It's the first step toward healing."

They sat in the fading light, the forest around them quiet and serene. Althea's presence felt like a balm to Emethy's wounded spirit, and for the first time in a while, she felt a glimmer of hope.

Back at the castle, Rian and Kellen were still reeling from the argument. Kellen paced the room, frustration etched on his face. "We need to fix this, Rian. We can't let this tear us apart."

Rian sighed, running a hand through his hair. "I know. I just... I didn't understand. But I want to. I want to make things right."

The two friends shared a determined look. They knew the road ahead would be challenging, but they were willing to walk it together, for Emethy's sake.

As night fell, Althea and Emethy made their way back to the castle. The air was cool, and the stars began to twinkle above. Althea glanced at Emethy, seeing a newfound strength in her eyes.

"We'll take this one step at a time," Althea said. "You're not alone, Emethy. Remember that."

Emethy nodded, her heart lighter than it had been in days. She was ready to face whatever came next, with her friends by her side. And with Althea's wise words echoing in her mind, she knew she had the strength to overcome any obstacle

The night sky over the Dim Light Castle was a sea of stars, their distant light barely piercing the thick darkness that loomed over the forest. A chill in the air foreshadowed the coming danger, and the uneasy silence was soon shattered by the roar of a monstrous creature, a harbinger of destruction sent by the king.

Emethy, Kellen, and Rian had barely begun to unwind from the night's earlier battle when the creature struck. Its grotesque form was barely visible against the inky blackness of the forest, but its growls and roars were unmistakable. The castle's walls trembled with each approaching step.

"Get ready!" Kellen shouted, grabbing his bow and notching an arrow. Rian readied his sword, his face set in determination. Emethy, still recovering from her previous injuries, took a deep breath and summoned her power, feeling the familiar tug of the wind and water within her.

As the creature emerged from the shadows, it was clear that this was not an ordinary beast. Its eyes glowed with a malevolent fire, and its movements were both erratic and fearsome. Kellen and Rian engaged the creature with all their might, their attacks meeting the beast with a clash of steel and fury.

Emethy joined the fray, her hands weaving through the air as she summoned powerful gusts of wind and waves of water. She tried to use her abilities to distract and disorient the creature, but the beast's rage made it relentless.

Desperate to gain an upper hand, Emethy reached out with her senses, using her connection to the wind and water to send a plea for help to the creature she had encountered in the forest. She focused on the memories of their previous encounter, hoping the message would reach him.

"Please, help us! The creature attacking us is in need of compassion. She is not what she seems."

Her message traveled through the wind and water, weaving a path through the forest. After what seemed like an eternity, the familiar figure of the father creature emerged from the darkness, his massive form cutting through the underbrush with purpose.

The father creature's arrival brought a glimmer of hope to the beleaguered group. As he approached, he realized with horror that the creature attacking them was his own daughter, transformed into a monster by the king's dark magic. His heart ached at the sight of his child's distorted form, and he roared in anguish.

Emethy, Kellen, and Rian fell back, their fight momentarily paused as the father creature and his daughter clashed. The two creatures fought fiercely, their roars and snarls echoing through the forest. The father creature's efforts to subdue his daughter were desperate and sorrowful.

With every strike, the father creature tried to reach the child within the monster. "My daughter, stop! It is me, your father. You are not a monster. You were made to suffer, but you are still my child!"

The daughter creature's monstrous form hesitated, her rage faltering as she heard her father's voice. The battle between them slowed as the father creature managed to approach her. With tears in his eyes, he reached out and gently cradled her monstrous face.

"Please, remember who you are. You are not monstrous. You are my beloved child."

As the father creature's words reached her, the daughter's monstrous features began to fade. The fight became a heartbreaking struggle between father and daughter. The glow of the full moon illuminated the scene, casting an ethereal light over the clearing.

Emethy's birthmark, glowing brightly in the moonlight, added an otherworldly glow to the scene. The golden light from Emethy's birthmark seemed to enhance the father creature's attempt to restore his daughter's true form.

In a final, tender moment, the daughter creature's monstrous appearance dissipated entirely. The beast's form reverted to that of a frightened, innocent girl, her eyes filled with both fear and recognition. Her father's arms held her gently as she took her last breath, her spirit freeing itself from the corrupted form.

The daughter's spirit, now free from the monstrous transformation, floated upward, glowing softly. The father creature watched, his grief palpable as his child's spirit ascended to the heavens. He roared in defiance at the king's cruelty, vowing vengeance against the one who had wrought such suffering.

Emethy, Kellen, and Rian stood silently, witnessing the tragic reunion. The night air was thick with the weight of loss and sorrow. The father creature, still trembling with anger and sadness, turned to Emethy.

"Tell me what must be done," he demanded, his voice heavy with pain. "I want to avenge my daughter. But I will not act until we know the king's weakness."

Emethy looked at the father creature with empathy. "We need to gather more information about the king's power. Only then can we plan our next move."

Althea, who had arrived during the conflict, placed a hand on Emethy's shoulder, her face a mask of sorrow and resolve. "You did well, Emethy. It was a terrible night, but we will find a way to end this suffering."

The father creature nodded solemnly. "I will bide my time. My daughter's spirit deserves justice, and so does the kingdom. We will find the king's weakness, and we will make him pay for what he has done."

With the dawn breaking, the group returned to the castle, their spirits weighed down by the night's events. The battle had been fierce, but it had also revealed the deep ties of family and the devastating effects of the king's magic. As they prepared for the challenges ahead, they knew that their quest was far from over.

Chapter 15

Forging the Path

&

Echoes of Strategy

After the battle, the castle fell into a tense silence, each member retreating to their quarters, exhausted and deep in thought. The shadows of the past few days lingered, and the air was thick with unresolved tensions and unspoken fears.

The next day, they all gathered in the main hall, the weight of their mission pressing down on them. Althea stood at the head of the table, her gaze steady and commanding. "We need to make a plan to defeat the king once and for all. If we don't, he will continue to send his forces after Emethy."

Kellen nodded, his jaw set with determination. "We need to find his weakness. There must be something that can tip the scales in our favor."

Rian, though still nursing a grudge, added, "We need to be stronger, more prepared. We can't afford any more surprises."

Emethy listened intently, though her mind was elsewhere. Every night, when the castle was quiet and everyone else was asleep, she heard faint whispers carried by the wind and the rivers. They spoke of something hidden, something that belonged to her. She hadn't told anyone about these whispers yet, choosing instead to ponder their meaning in silence.

There was a lot going on inside Emethy's head. The memory of the butcher, the revelation of her powers, and the growing pressure of their mission weighed heavily on her. She felt a mixture of fear and determination, uncertainty and resolve.

During the day, Emethy sought out Althea, asking her to teach her more spells and magical techniques. Althea, seeing the determination in Emethy's eyes, agreed to help. "You have potential, Emethy. But you must focus. Harness your power."

Every day, Emethy practiced diligently, honing her skills in both combat and magic. She learned to channel her energy more effectively, to cast spells with greater precision, and to tap into the power of her birthmark. The others, too, dedicated themselves to improving their abilities. Kellen trained tirelessly with his weapons, Rian worked on his strategy and agility, and even Ploma found ways to contribute, her presence bringing a sense of normalcy and comfort to the group.

At night, when the castle was quiet and everyone else was asleep, Emethy continued to hear the whispers. They spoke of something hidden, something that called to her. She couldn't shake the feeling that whatever it was, it was important—perhaps even crucial to their mission.

One particularly quiet night, as the moonlight streamed through her window, Emethy sat up in bed, straining to hear the whispers more clearly. They seemed to be guiding her, leading her to a place she couldn't yet see. The mystery of it all was both intriguing and unsettling.

Emethy decided to keep this information to herself for now, not wanting to worry the others or distract them from their training. Instead, she focused on learning as much as she could from Althea during the day. She absorbed every lesson, every spell, every piece of advice with an intensity that surprised even herself.

Meanwhile, the rest of the group continued to enhance their skills. Kellen and Rian sparred daily, pushing each other to new limits. Ploma, though not as skilled in combat, found ways to support the group, ensuring they had everything they needed. Althea, with her vast knowledge and experience, guided them all, her presence a steadying force.

Despite the growing tension and the looming threat of the king's next move, there was a sense of camaraderie and purpose among them. They were no longer just individuals brought together by circumstance; they were a team, united by a common goal.

Emethy felt a growing connection to her friends, a bond forged in the heat of battle and the quiet moments in between. Yet, the whispers continued to haunt her, a constant reminder that there was still much she didn't know, much she needed to discover.

As the days turned into weeks, Emethy's determination only grew stronger. She knew that whatever the whispers were leading her to, it was something she had to find. And with the support of her friends, she was more determined than ever to uncover the secrets that lay hidden, to understand her true power, and to defeat the king once and for all.

The path ahead was uncertain, but Emethy felt a glimmer of hope. She was no longer the frightened girl who had fled from her village; she was a warrior, a leader, and a beacon of hope. And with her friends by her side, she was ready to face whatever challenges awaited them.

The forest was thick with shadows as Rian made his way through the dense foliage, his thoughts heavy with the weight of their mission. The air was cool, and the soft rustling of leaves provided a soothing backdrop to his contemplations. He was far from the castle, seeking solitude and clarity.
But the tranquility of the forest was deceiving. Without warning, a group of the king's combatants ambushed Rian. They moved with practiced stealth and efficiency, their faces obscured by dark hoods. Rian fought valiantly, his skills honed from countless battles, but the sheer number of his attackers overwhelmed him. After a fierce struggle, he was subdued and dragged away into the depths of the forest.

Back at the castle, the absence of Rian was immediately noticed. Panic spread through the group as they scoured the surrounding area, calling out his name. Hours turned into a desperate search, but there was no trace of him. Anxiety gnawed at their hearts, fear for their friend's safety mingling with the dread of what his capture might mean.

Emethy felt a rising tide of panic and determination. She closed her eyes and focused, reaching out with her senses. The wind carried faint whispers, and for the first time, she tried to manipulate it. Concentrating intensely, she willed the wind to bring her information, to reveal what had happened to Rian.

To her astonishment, the wind obeyed. It carried the voices of the trees, the rustling leaves, the murmurs of distant streams. She could hear snippets of conversations, the echo of footsteps, and finally, the chilling confirmation of Rian's fate. The king's combatants had taken him, intending to use him as leverage to force Emethy to surrender.

She opened her eyes, her heart pounding with the revelation. The others looked at her expectantly, sensing that she had learned something significant.

"Rian has been taken by the king's men," she said, her voice steady despite the turmoil inside her. "They want me to surrender."
Kellen's face darkened with anger. "We can't let that happen. We have to get him back."

Althea, ever the strategist, placed a calming hand on Kellen's shoulder. "We need a plan. We can't rush into this blindly."
Emethy nodded, feeling a surge of determination. "I can manipulate the wind. I can gather information. We'll use every resource we have to find him and bring him back."

For the first time, Emethy's newfound ability felt like a beacon of hope rather than a burden. She closed her eyes again, this time with purpose, directing the wind to seek out Rian's location. The whispers grew louder, more distinct, guiding her thoughts.

"They're holding him in a secluded camp," she said, her voice filled with certainty. "Not far from the king's fortress. We need to move quickly."
With renewed resolve, the group gathered their weapons and supplies, readying themselves for the rescue mission. Althea outlined their strategy, her calm demeanor instilling confidence in the others. Ploma, though not a fighter, offered to stay behind and prepare for their return, ensuring they had a safe place to regroup.

As they moved out, Emethy felt a mixture of fear and determination. The thought of Rian in the king's clutches was unbearable, but she knew they had the strength and unity to rescue him. The wind whispered encouragement, its ethereal voice a reminder of her growing power and the hope that lay within.

The journey to the king's camp was swift but tense. Emethy used her wind manipulation to scout ahead, avoiding patrols and detecting traps. The group's movements were synchronized, each member playing a crucial role in their advance.

Finally, they reached the outskirts of the camp. Hidden in the shadows, they observed the layout and the positions of the guards. Emethy directed the wind to carry her message to Rian, reassuring him that help was on the way.

The rescue mission was a blur of action and stealth. Kellen and Althea led the charge, taking down guards with swift precision. Emethy focused on using her abilities to create distractions and clear paths. The sound of clashing swords and muffled cries filled the night, but the group remained undeterred.

Back at the castle, they regrouped, their bond stronger than ever. They knew the road ahead would be fraught with danger, but together, they were determined to face whatever challenges came their way. For now, they had a moment of respite, a chance to heal and plan their next move. And Emethy, with her growing powers, was ready to lead them into the unknown.

The morning was gray and misty as the group gathered in the castle's main hall. The previous night's events had left everyone on edge, and the weight of their mission pressed heavily upon them. They were determined to rescue Rian from the king's clutches and put an end to his reign of terror.

Emethy stood by the window, her thoughts racing. Her newfound abilities with the wind had proven invaluable, but the challenge ahead was immense. The king was relentless, and the danger they faced was greater than ever. She turned to the others, her gaze settling on Kellen and the father creature, Gorath, who had become their unlikely ally.

"We can't wait any longer," Emethy said, her voice steady. "We need to strike now, while we have the element of surprise."

Kellen nodded, his expression serious. "We'll go with you, Emethy. Gorath's strength and knowledge of the forest will be our advantage."

Gorath, the once-menacing creature who had now become their ally, stepped forward. His eyes, once filled with sorrow for his lost daughter, now burned with determination. "The palace is heavily guarded, but there are secret paths only I know. We can use them to our advantage."

Althea looked up from the map, her expression firm. "You must be cautious. The king's men will be on high alert after Rian's capture. Stick to the shadows, and trust in each other."

With final preparations complete, Emethy, Kellen, and Gorath set out into the misty morning. The forest seemed to close in around them, its silence both a comfort and a threat. Emethy led the way, her senses heightened, the wind whispering guidance.

As they travelled, Gorath shared stories of the palace's defences and its hidden passages. "The king's fortress is vast, but there are weaknesses," he explained. "Underground tunnels, forgotten corridors... places only those who once served the king would know."
Kellen listened intently, his mind focused on the task ahead. "We need to be careful. The king won't expect us to come through these paths, but that doesn't mean they won't be guarded."

Emethy nodded, her eyes scanning the forest for any signs of danger. The journey was arduous, and the terrain grew more challenging as they neared the palace. Thick underbrush and treacherous paths slowed their progress, but Gorath's guidance was invaluable.

As Emethy scanned the forest ahead, her breath caught. For a fleeting moment, a shadow loomed in the distance, dark and formless, watching. It disappeared as quickly as it appeared, leaving her unsure if it was real or just her mind playing tricks—but the unease it left behind lingered.

As night fell, they set up a small, concealed camp. Emethy sat by the fire, her thoughts drifting to the challenges ahead. The wind whispered around her, carrying faint echoes of the palace and the king's sinister plans. She felt a surge of determination. They would succeed.

"Tomorrow, we reach the palace," Gorath said, his deep voice breaking the silence. "The final stretch will be the most dangerous."

Kellen placed a reassuring hand on Emethy's shoulder. "We'll get through this, together."

The next morning, they continued their journey, the palace's dark silhouette looming in the distance. The air grew colder, and an eerie stillness settled over the forest.

As they approached the outer walls, Gorath led them to a hidden entrance, overgrown with vines and barely visible.

"This is it," Gorath whispered. "Stay close and stay quiet."

They slipped through the entrance, the passage narrow and damp. The air was thick with tension as they navigated the underground tunnels, each step bringing them closer to their goal.

Finally, they emerged in a forgotten corridor within the palace walls. The air was musty, and the flickering torchlight cast eerie shadows on the stone walls. Emethy took a deep breath, her heart pounding. The real battle was about to begin.

"We need to find Rian and the weapon the king guards so fiercely," Kellen whispered. "Stay alert."

Emethy nodded, her senses on high alert. The corridors were a maze, but Gorath's knowledge guided them. They moved swiftly and silently, avoiding patrols and listening for any signs of Rian.

Emethy and Kellen slipped through the narrow corridors of the king's fortress, their footsteps barely a whisper against the stone. The dim glow of torchlight cast long shadows as they approached the Commission Chamber. Hiding behind a massive pillar, they peered into the room. Guards lined the walls, oblivious to their presence, but the weight of danger hung thick in the air. Emethy steadied her breath, her heart pounding as she exchanged a tense glance with Kellen.

The grand doors of the Hall of Commission loomed before Rian, their intricate carvings depicting scenes of judgment and punishment. The guards flanking him pushed the heavy doors open, and Rian was led into the vast chamber, where the air was thick with the scent of burning incense and old parchment.
At the far end of the hall, seated on a raised dais, was the King, his expression a mask of stern resolve. Beside him were the members of the Commission, a council of grim-faced men and women known for their ruthless methods of extracting the truth.

Rian's heart pounded in his chest, but he forced himself to walk with steady steps. His mind raced with the events that had led him here. The accusations were clear: he had allegedly aided in the escape of Seraphina, the traitor. Though he knew the truth, he also knew that convincing the Commission of his innocence would be nearly impossible.
"Rian of Aeloria," the King's voice echoed through the chamber, "you stand accused of aiding the traitor's escape. What do you have to say in your defense?"

Rian bowed deeply, his eyes meeting the King's for a brief moment before he spoke. "Your Majesty, I swear by all that is sacred, I did not help Seraphina. I did not even know of her escape until it was too late."

The King's gaze hardened. "And yet, evidence suggests otherwise. You were seen near the cells on the night she escaped. You have been seen conversing with individuals who are now under suspicion."

Rian's mind flashed back to that night. He had indeed been near the cells, but it was a mere coincidence. He had been searching for Emethy, fearing for her safety after the disturbances in the palace. His association with those now under suspicion was circumstantial at best.

"My presence near the cells was purely coincidental, Your Majesty," Rian pleaded. "I was looking for Emethy. I feared she might be in danger. As for those I have spoken with, I had no knowledge of their intentions."

The King motioned to the head of the Commission, a tall, gaunt man with piercing eyes. "Proceed," he commanded.

The head of the Commission stepped forward, his voice cold and devoid of emotion. "Rian of Aeloria, you are to be subjected to the tools of truth. If you speak the truth, you will have nothing to fear. If you lie, your suffering will be your own doing."

Rian was dragged to a large wooden table in the center of the hall, where various instruments of torture were laid out. His wrists were shackled, and he was forced to kneel on the cold stone floor. The head of the Commission selected a thin, barbed whip and approached Rian.
"Confess, and this will end quickly," the man whispered, though his eyes held no promise of mercy.

Rian clenched his jaw, determined to withstand whatever pain was inflicted upon him. He knew the truth, and he would not betray his friends or his own honor by admitting to something he had not done.
The first lash of the whip tore through his tunic and flesh, and Rian gritted his teeth to stifle a cry. The pain was searing, but he refused to break. Each subsequent strike was a test of his resolve, but with each lash, he reminded himself of Emethy and Kellan. He could not let them down.

Minutes felt like hours, and Rian's back was a tapestry of agony. The head of the Commission paused, inspecting his handiwork before leaning close to Rian's ear. "The truth, Rian. Tell us who helped Seraphina."

Rian's voice was hoarse, but it held firm. "I did not help her. I know nothing."

The whip lashed out again, and Rian's vision blurred. He felt himself teetering on the edge of consciousness, but a fierce determination kept him from succumbing. He would not betray his friends.

The King watched in silence, his expression unreadable. After what felt like an eternity, he raised his hand, signaling the head of the Commission to stop. The hall fell silent, save for Rian's ragged breathing.

The King stood and addressed the hall. "Enough. His punishment is complete. Let this serve as a warning to all who think to defy the crown."

Rian was unshackled and dragged to the edge of the hall, his body battered and broken, but his spirit unyielding. As he was taken away, he caught a glimpse of Emethy hidden in the shadows, her eyes filled with a mix of sorrow and determination. He had withstood the Commission's torture, but he knew the fight was far from over. He was sent back to the chamber.

Emethy held up her hand, signaling for them to stop. She listened intently, the wind carrying faint words to her ears. It was Rian, and he was close.

"This way," she whispered, leading them down another dark corridor.

They approached a heavy wooden door, and Gorath carefully pressed his ear against it. "He's inside," he confirmed.

Kellen drew his sword, ready for whatever lay beyond. Emethy felt a surge of determination as she placed her hand on the door, the wind swirling around her in anticipation. With a nod from Gorath, she pushed the door open, and they stepped into the chamber.

Rian was shackled to the wall, his face bruised and battered. He looked up, his eyes widening in surprise and relief as he saw them.

"Emethy... Kellen..." he rasped.

"We're here to get you out," Emethy said, her voice filled with resolve.

Gorath moved quickly, breaking Rian's shackles with his immense strength. Kellen helped Rian to his feet, supporting him as they prepared to leave.

"Let's move," Gorath urged. "We don't have much time."

As they made their way back through the corridors, the palace began to stir with the realization that intruders were within its walls. The air was thick with tension, and every shadow seemed to hold a threat.

But Emethy, Kellen, Gorath, and Rian pressed on, their determination unwavering. They had come too far to turn back now. The king's reign of terror would soon come to an end, and they would see to it.

Finally, they emerged from the palace, the cool night air a welcome relief. The journey ahead was still fraught with danger, but for now, they had each other and the strength to face whatever came next.

As they disappeared into the forest, the palace behind them loomed ominously, a dark reminder of the battle still to come. But Emethy knew that together, they would prevail. The wind whispered promises of victory, and she believed in them with all her heart.

The moon hung low in the sky as the group made their way through the dense forest. The shadows seemed to shift and twist with every step, a reminder of the king's malevolent presence. Rian, weakened but determined, walked between Emethy and Kellen, leaning on them for support.

"We need to find a safe place to rest," Gorath rumbled, his eyes scanning the darkened woods. "The king's men will be searching for us."

Emethy nodded, her senses heightened. The wind carried whispers of danger, and she knew they had to be cautious. "There's a clearing ahead," she said, her voice barely above a whisper. "We can set up camp there."

As they reached the clearing, Emethy and Kellen helped Rian to a makeshift bed of leaves and blankets. Gorath stood guard, his massive form a comforting presence in the darkness. The night was quiet, but an unsettling feeling lingered in the air.

Emethy sat beside Rian, her heart heavy with worry. "How are you feeling?" she asked softly.

Rian managed a weak smile. "I've been better," he replied. "But I'm glad to be out of that place."

Kellen knelt beside them, his expression serious. "We'll get you back to Althea," he said firmly. "She'll know how to help you."

As the night wore on, the group settled into an uneasy sleep. Emethy's dreams were filled with dark visions of the king and his twisted plans. She woke with a start, her heart pounding. The wind whispered urgent warnings, and she knew something was wrong.

Suddenly, Rian began to convulse, his body writhing in pain. Emethy and Kellen rushed to his side, their faces etched with fear. "What's happening?" Kellen cried, trying to hold Rian still.

Emethy's eyes widened as she realized the truth. "It's a spell," she whispered. "The king must have placed it on him."

Gorath moved closer, his expression grim. "We need to break it, or he'll die."

Emethy's mind raced. She reached out with her powers, feeling the currents of the wind and the whispers of the forest. But the spell was strong, and her abilities were not enough to counter it.

"I can't... I can't break it," she said, tears filling her eyes. "It's too powerful."

Rian's convulsions grew weaker, his breaths coming in ragged gasps. Emethy held his hand, her heart breaking. "Stay with us, Rian," she pleaded. "Please, stay with us."

But it was too late. With one final shudder, Rian's body went still. The forest seemed to hold its breath, the silence deafening. Emethy's sobs broke the stillness, her grief overwhelming.

Kellen placed a hand on her shoulder, his own eyes filled with tears. "He's gone," he said softly.

Emethy's sorrow quickly turned to anger. She stood, her eyes blazing with determination. "This isn't over," she said, her voice trembling with rage. "The king will pay for this."

Gorath nodded, his own grief mirrored in his eyes. "We'll see to it," he said. "But we need a plan."

Emethy took a deep breath, her resolve hardening. "We march back to the palace," she said. "Tonight."

Kellen and Gorath exchanged glances, then nodded in agreement. They quickly gathered their supplies, preparing for the journey back. The night was dark, but Emethy's anger burned brightly, guiding them forward.

She would not rest until the king was defeated and Rian's death avenged.

The palace loomed ahead, its dark silhouette a symbol of the evil they faced. Emethy's heart pounded with a mix of fear and determination. They would confront the king, and they would win. For Rian, and for everyone who had suffered under the king's rule.

As they reached the palace gates, Emethy felt a surge of energy. The wind swirled around her, carrying promises of victory. She looked at Kellen and Gorath, their faces set with resolve. Together, they would bring an end to the king's reign of terror.

And with that, they stepped into the darkness, ready to face whatever lay ahead.

Chapter 16

The Sword of Destiny

&

The Shadow of Death

Emethy's heart pounded as they reached the palace. The dark structure loomed ahead, its walls tall and foreboding. Shadows danced across the stone, and an eerie silence filled the air. Emethy's senses were heightened, every nerve on edge.

As they crept through the palace corridors, the whispers of the wind grew stronger, guiding Emethy towards a hidden chamber. She felt a pull, a connection that she couldn't ignore. "This way," she whispered to Kellen and Gorath.

They moved swiftly, avoiding patrols and slipping through shadowed passages. Finally, they reached a large, ornate door. Emethy's birthmark tingled, glowing faintly. She pushed the door open and stepped inside.

The chamber was dimly lit, and at its center stood a pedestal holding an ancient sword. The blade was long and gleaming, etched with intricate runes. Emethy approached it, her birthmark glowing brighter as she neared the weapon.

"This is it," she murmured, reaching out to grasp the hilt. The moment her fingers touched the sword, a surge of energy coursed through her. The runes on the blade glowed, matching the pattern of her birthmark.

Kellen and Gorath watched in awe as Emethy lifted the sword. It was heavy, but she felt a strange familiarity with it, as if it had always been hers. The connection was undeniable.

"We have the weapon," Kellen said, his voice filled with hope. "Now, we face the king."

They moved quickly, the sword giving them a newfound sense of purpose. But as they made their way through the palace, they encountered the king's combatants. The clash of steel echoed through the halls as they fought their way forward.

Emethy swung the sword with precision, the blade cutting through the air with ease. Kellen fought beside her, his movements fluid and fierce despite his injuries. Gorath used his immense strength to fend off attackers, but the battle was intense.

Suddenly, the king appeared, his presence overwhelming. He moved with a crooked gait, his eyes filled with malice. With a wave of his hand, he cast a spell, freezing Gorath in place.

"Stay back!" Emethy shouted, but it was too late. Gorath was immobilized, his face twisted in frustration.

Kellen, already injured, struggled to keep up the fight. "Emethy, be careful!" he called out, trying to protect her.

The king laughed, his voice cold and mocking. "You think you can defeat me? Foolish girl."

Emethy's grip tightened on the sword. She felt the energy pulsing through it, the connection between the blade and her birthmark strengthening. "This ends now," she said, her voice steady.

The king lunged at her, his own dark magic crackling around him. Emethy met his attack head-on, the sword glowing with power. Their blades clashed, and sparks flew. Emethy could feel the king's malevolence, but she pushed back with all her might.

Kellen fought off the remaining combatants, but he was weakening. "Emethy, you have to finish this!" he shouted, desperation in his voice.

Emethy focused on the king, blocking out everything else. She channelled her anger, her grief for Rian, and her determination to end the king's reign. With a powerful swing, she struck the king's blade, shattering it.

The king stumbled back, shock and rage contorting his features. "Impossible!" he hissed.

The corridors of the palace were filled with tension as Emethystin, Kellen, and Gorath were escorted to the Hall of Commission. The heavy tread of the king's Guards echoed ominously, their faces impassive and cold. Emethy's injuries were severe, her body aching with each step, but her grip on the Sword of Destiny was firm.

As they entered the grand hall, the atmosphere was oppressive. The king, seated on a darkened throne, watched them with a smug, cruel satisfaction. His eyes glinted with malevolent glee as he took in the sight of his captives.

"You've come a long way, Emethystin," the king said, his voice dripping with disdain. "But this is where it ends."Fdarion

Emethy's strength was waning. She could barely keep herself upright, her vision blurring with pain. Kellen, despite his own injuries, stood by her side, his face set in a grim line. Gorath loomed beside them, his imposing figure a stark contrast to the king's cruel demeanor.

The king raised his hand, and the air seemed to crackle with dark energy. "Bring them closer," he commanded.

The Guards moved forward, dragging Emethy, Kellen, and Gorath towards the center of the hall. The large chamber was filled with the king's elite guard, their armor gleaming menacingly in the dim light.

Emethy tightened her grip on the sword, its runes glowing faintly. She knew that this was their last stand, but she was determined to make it count. The weight of the sword seemed to grow heavier with each step, but she refused to let it fall.

Suddenly, the king's dark magic surged through the room, swirling around Emethy and her friends. She fought to keep her balance, her breath coming in ragged gasps. The king's voice echoed, a chilling incantation that seemed to sap their strength.

Emethy's knees buckled, and she fell to the floor, her vision fading. She could hear the distant sounds of Kellen and Gorath fighting back, but it was all becoming a blur. The king's spell was overwhelming, and the darkness was closing in.

As the king's massive personal bodyguard approached, sword raised high, Emethy's strength finally gave out. The immense blade swung down towards her, a final, decisive strike.

In that moment, as the sword was about to descend, a dark image materialized before the bodyguard. It was an ethereal figure, shadowy and imposing, with eyes that glowed with an intense, otherworldly light. The figure seemed to emanate a powerful, protective aura, its presence filling the hall with an unsettling darkness.

The bodyguard halted mid-swing, his eyes widening in shock as the dark image loomed before him. The hall fell into an eerie silence, the only sound the distant hum of dark magic.

Emethy lay on the cold floor, her strength fading, her mind barely conscious of the chaos around her. The dark figure hovered, its gaze fixed on the king, and a sense of foreboding filled the chamber.

As the figure continued to loom over the scene, the tension in the hall was palpable. The king's expression shifted from triumph to confusion and fear, his eyes darting between the figure and Emethy.

The chapter ends with the dark image standing guard over Emethy, the final confrontation poised on the brink of an unknown resolution. The fate of Emethy, Kellen, and Gorath hangs in the balance, as the darkness envelops them all.

The darkness of the Hall of Commission was pierced by a blinding light as the dark figure, cloaked in shadow, revealed itself to be Death. The figure's eyes, hidden beneath the hood, emanated a chilling aura that seemed to freeze the very air in the room.

In a single, fluid motion, Death swung a blade, its edge glinting with an otherworldly sheen. The massive bodyguard and the king's Guards fell in a cascade of lifeless bodies, their forms collapsing before the king. The scene was so swift and efficient that it left a palpable silence in its wake. The king, his face a mask of shock and fear, could only manage to utter a single word.

"Death."

To Emethy, the figure's presence was eerily familiar. Despite the hood obscuring its face, she felt a deep, unsettling connection. The very essence of Death seemed to resonate with the core of her being, stirring something within her.

As Emethy lay injured on the cold floor, her birthmark flared with a brilliant light. The sword she had been wielding pulsed with a powerful energy, as though it were alive. The merging of her power with the blade filled her with a renewed strength. With a fierce determination, she rose, her movements fuelled by the radiant glow of her birthmark and the sword's divine energy.

The king, struggling to regain his composure, attempted to cast spells and commands, but Emethy's newfound strength overwhelmed him. With a decisive swing of her sword, she struck down the king, ending his reign of terror. The palace walls trembled as the light of the sword pierced through the darkness, marking the end of a tyrant's rule.

As the king's immobile body crumpled to the ground breathing ploddingly, the dark figure, Death, began to fade into the shadows. The remaining light cast eerie shapes across the walls, the sense of ominous finality hanging heavy in the air. The palace, now a silent witness to the battle, seemed to hold its breath as Death departed.

The prince, arriving in the aftermath of the chaos, surveyed the destruction with a mix of horror and disbelief. His eyes fixed on Emethy, he struggled to comprehend the scene before him. Without full knowledge of his father's dark intentions or the true nature of the battle, he pointed an accusatory finger at Emethy.

"You!" the prince shouted, his voice laced with anger and confusion. "You've brought this upon us! You're responsible for this massacre!"

Emethy, her strength waning and her injuries still fresh, chose to ignore the prince's accusations. Her focus was on escape, on leaving the palace that had become a symbol of her suffering. She knew that any explanation would be futile in the face of such overwhelming misunderstanding.

Gorath, his form towering and steadfast, carried Emethy with careful strength. Despite his own injuries, he moved with a determined resolve. Kellen, though wounded, supported the two of them as they made their way out of the palace, the weight of their recent ordeal settling heavily upon them.

As they exited into the cool night air, Kellen's mind raced with questions. The appearance of Death, the intervention, and the choice to save them rather than exacting further destruction puzzled him. Why would

Death, a force of inevitable finality, choose to save them instead of sealing their fates?

Their escape from the palace was shrouded in the quiet of the night, their path illuminated only by the faint glow of Emethy's birthmark and the moonlight. The questions and uncertainties loomed large, but for now, they found solace in their departure from the palace and the immediate danger that had threatened their lives.

Kellen, as they moved further from the palace, couldn't shake the image of Death's presence from his mind. He knew that their journey was far from over, and the true motives behind Death's intervention were yet to be revealed. As they walked into the unknown, the weight of their past actions and the uncertainties of the future intertwined, forging a path that they would have to navigate together.

The sun had sunk beneath the horizon, casting an eerie glow across the landscape as Emethy approached the place where Dim Light Castle once stood. Her heart pounded with a mix of anticipation and dread. The towering structure, a constant shadow in her memory, was gone. Not a single trace remained, as though it had never existed.

Her eyes swept the barren landscape in disbelief. Althea was gone too, vanished like a whisper in the wind. The place where they had once spoken, where plans had been made, where secrets were kept, now felt like a hollow dream.

"How can this be?" Emethy murmured, gripping the hilt of her sword. A gust of cold wind blew past her, sending a shiver down her spine. Something was wrong. The world around her was quieter than it should be, and the forest that once teemed with life now felt suffocated by an unseen force.

She stepped forward, her feet crunching against the dried leaves. Her mind raced, trying to piece together where Althea could have gone and why the castle had disappeared. In the back of her mind, a familiar unease stirred — a voice she had silenced time and time again. The connection between Althea and the Dark Shadow of Death lingered in her thoughts, though she had always pushed it aside.

"No," she thought, shaking her head. "There must be another explanation."

Lyra hovered beside her, biting her lip. "Emethy... it's gone," she whispered, her small, translucent form flickering in the fading light. Emethy's jaw clenched as she scanned the desolate horizon, the birthmark on her shoulder glowing faintly, responding to the ancient forces around her.

"They were waiting for me," Emethy muttered, trying to make sense of the situation. "Something's not right."

But the deeper truth gnawed at her—a connection between Althea and the dark shadows of death, an understanding she had been running from for too long. "No", she told herself. "It's not true". Yet the unease curled inside her, growing stronger, impossible to ignore.

"Emethy, what do we do now?" Lyra asked, her voice laced with fear. "Should we keep looking?"

Emethy hesitated, looking down at the glowing sigil on her shoulder. The faint warmth pulsing from it seemed to suggest otherwise. She closed her eyes briefly, gathering her thoughts. "No. We return."

"To your aunt?" Lyra's eyes widened. "But the Crooked King—he's still after you. He won't stop."

Emethy nodded grimly. "I know. He's relentless. But I need answers, and Aunt Merella is the only one who might have them. There's more at play here than just him."

The mention of the Crooked King sent a shiver down her spine. Emethy knew he was furious, burning with hatred for her, his plans of destruction far from abandoned. She could feel his rage like a dark cloud lingering in the distance, waiting to strike again. But there was something more—something deeper that tied Althea to the Dark Shadow of Death, something Emethy wasn't ready to face.

She swallowed hard. "We need to be prepared for what's coming."

Lyra nodded, sensing Emethy's resolve. The two turned their backs to the empty land where Dim Light Castle had once stood and started the long trek through the forest, the air thick with uncertainty.

As they walked, a chill settled in the air, and the shadows seemed to grow longer, darker, as though something unseen watched them from afar. The whispers of the wind felt sharper now, more urgent, carrying a warning Emethy couldn't quite decipher.

When they finally reached the edge of the forest, Emethy paused, her mind racing. She looked down at her birthmark, which had begun to glow brighter in the encroaching darkness.

"Aunt Merella will know what to do," she whispered, more to herself than to Lyra. But deep down, she wasn't sure. There were too many unanswered questions—about Althea, about the shadows that followed her, and about the path that lay ahead.

Emethy's journey was far from over. She could feel it—this was only the beginning of something much darker, much more dangerous.

As the moonlight flickered through the trees, casting twisted shadows on the ground, Emethy knew the truth would soon come to light. But when it did, she wasn't sure she'd be ready to face it.

The wind whispered again, carrying with it a single word that echoed in her mind, chilling her to the core.

"Death."

Her journey was far from finished. And the dark road ahead promised more secrets, more enemies, and more shadows waiting to rise.

With Lyra beside her, Emethy stepped forward, the weight of what was to come pressing heavily on her shoulders.

"Every ending carries the whispers of a new beginning—unwritten, uncertain, yet waiting for the brave to turn the page."

Chapter 17

The Crossroads of Change

The village of **Thistledown** had become a haven for **Emethy**, a place where she could find fleeting moments of peace. The people had come to know her as the healer, the one who mended not just broken bones but broken spirits. Her days were filled with the comforting rhythm of life: tending to the wounded, gathering herbs in the forest, and spending quiet evenings with her aunt. It was a simplicity she cherished, though she knew it could never last.

One crisp morning, Emethy ventured into the bustling flea market at the village square. The air was alive with chatter, the clinking of coins, and the aroma of freshly baked bread. She browsed the stalls, her fingers brushing over colorful fabrics and trinkets, her heart lighter than it had been in months.

As the sun dipped lower in the sky, casting long shadows over the cobbled streets, Emethy began her walk back home. The forest path was quiet, save for the crunch of leaves beneath her boots. She was halfway through the winding trail when she felt it—a prickle at the back of her neck, the sensation of being watched.

She stopped, her hand instinctively reaching for the dagger at her belt. The trees around her stood silent, their branches swaying gently in the breeze. And then she saw it—a shadow, slipping between the trees, too large to be an animal. Her heart raced as she quickened her pace, refusing to glance back.

By the time she reached the safety of her aunt's home, the shadow was gone, but the unease lingered.

The next day, as Emethy went about her tasks, she couldn't shake the feeling of being followed. She told herself it was nothing, a trick of her mind. But when she returned to the clearing near the market, she saw him.

The prince.

Alaric stepped into the light, his hands raised in a gesture of peace. He was dressed simply, his royal demeanor softened, though his presence was impossible to ignore.

"Emethy," he said, his voice carrying a note of hesitance. "Please, hear me out."

Emethy's eyes narrowed, her grip tightening on her dagger. "What are you doing here?" she demanded.

"I'm not here to harm you," Alaric said quickly. "I've left the palace. I'm not like my father."

"You expect me to believe that?" she shot back, her voice cold.

Before Alaric could answer, another figure emerged from the trees. A tall man with chiseled features and piercing blue eyes. His armor gleamed faintly in the dappled light as he bowed slightly to Emethy, exuding an air of quiet confidence.

"This is Commander Darion," Alaric said. "He's my most trusted guard. He can vouch for me."

Darion inclined his head. "I've served the prince since he was a boy. I stand by his word, Lady Emethy."

Emethy's gaze flicked between the two men, her instincts screaming at her to walk away. But something in Alaric's eyes stopped her. There was a sincerity there, a vulnerability she hadn't expected.

"I don't trust you," she said bluntly, turning on her heel. "Stay away from me and my village."

For days, Alaric persisted. He appeared at the edges of the market, helped villagers with mundane tasks, and even brought offerings of rare herbs for her healing work. Despite herself, Emethy began to notice the effort he was making. He seemed different, softer, as though he truly wanted to prove himself.

Finally, one evening as she returned from tending to a wounded farmer, she found Alaric waiting near her home. This time, he didn't speak. He simply handed her a small pouch of medicinal roots she had been searching for.

"Why are you doing this?" she asked, her voice weary.

"Because I need to make things right," he replied.

Emethy studied him for a long moment before letting out a sigh. "Fine. But don't think for a moment that I've forgiven you."

A week later, Alaric was introduced to the villagers. Emethy told them he was a friend from her travels, never mentioning his royal lineage. The villagers welcomed him cautiously, and Alaric's charm began to win them over. He helped repair roofs, carried heavy loads, and even joined in the evening gatherings around the fire. Lyra, however, was less enchanted. When she first saw Alaric, she crossed her arms and floated near Emethy, her translucent form quivering with frustration. "You trust him too easily," she muttered, her voice tinged with jealousy. Emethy tried to brush it off, but Lyra's sulking grew more pronounced with each passing day. By the time Alaric started helping the villagers, Lyra had taken to glaring at him from a distance, her disapproval palpable.

For the first time in months, Emethy felt a sliver of hope. She began to trust him, though a small voice in the back of her mind warned her to stay on guard. Alaric's motives seemed pure, but the shadow of his father's tyranny loomed large.

Unbeknownst to her, Commander watched her closely, his eyes flickering with something unspoken. Alaric had begun to visit the village frequently, charming the villagers with his presence and seamlessly integrating into their lives. Lyra, however, continued to bristle at his every action, her jealousy and frustration with Emethy's growing trust bubbling just beneath the surface. The prince's motives remained shrouded in mystery, and though Emethy's heart began to soften, her instincts whispered that danger was closer than ever.

Emethy's heart softened, but her instincts whispered that danger was closer than ever.

The days turned into weeks, and Alaric's presence in Thistledown became almost routine. Villagers grew accustomed to his easy smile and willingness to lend a hand, though Emethy remained guarded. Her trust in him was fragile, like a porcelain vase teetering on the edge of a shelf.

Lyra, however, was less inclined to tolerate Alaric. She lingered near Emethy, her spectral form flitting about like a restless bird. Each time Alaric approached, Lyra's translucent eyes narrowed, and her silvery voice grew sharper.

"Why do you let him stay?" she whispered one evening as Emethy sat on the edge of her bed, unbraiding her hair. "You've seen what men like him are capable of."

Emethy sighed, her fingers stilling. "He's different, Lyra. Or at least he's trying to be."

Lyra folded her arms, floating a few inches above the ground. "You're being a fool. He's hiding something—I can feel it."

Emethy didn't respond. Deep down, she couldn't shake the nagging suspicion that Lyra was right.

It was a misty morning when Emethy decided to visit the outskirts of the forest. The village's usual chatter was muffled by the heavy fog that clung to the air. She carried a small satchel filled with herbs; her dagger strapped securely to her thigh. Lyra followed, though she kept her distance, her frustration with Emethy still palpable.

"You shouldn't be wandering alone," Lyra muttered.

"I'm not alone," Emethy replied, glancing over her shoulder. "You're here, aren't you?"

Lyra huffed but said no more.

As Emethy knelt to inspect a cluster of wildflowers, she felt the ground vibrate faintly beneath her. She froze, her hand hovering over the delicate petals. The vibration grew stronger, accompanied by the distant sound of hooves.

She stood quickly, her eyes scanning the treeline. Moments later, a figure on horseback emerged from the fog. It was Alaric. He dismounted gracefully, his boots crunching against the forest floor.

"What are you doing here?" Emethy asked, her voice tinged with irritation.

Alaric held up his hands, a wry smile playing on his lips. "I was looking for you. The villagers said you'd come this way."

"Why?"

"Because I wanted to talk to you," he said, stepping closer. "And because I thought you might need some company."

Lyra's ghostly form hovered just behind Emethy, her expression stormy. "As if she needs *your* company," she muttered, though only Emethy could hear her.

Emethy crossed her arms. "I'm fine on my own."

"You're stubborn, I'll give you that," Alaric said with a chuckle. "But even the strongest need allies."

Emethy's gaze softened, though she didn't let it show. "Allies?" she repeated. "Is that what you are?"

Alaric's expression grew serious. "I want to be. If you'll let me."

Before Emethy could respond, a low growl rumbled from the shadows. Both she and Alaric turned toward the sound. From the dense underbrush, a pair of glowing eyes appeared, followed by the hulking form of a wolf-like creature. Its fur was black as coal, and its teeth gleamed like polished ivory.

Emethy drew her dagger instinctively, placing herself between the beast and Alaric. Lyra darted to her side, her ethereal glow dimming as fear flickered across her face.

"Stay back," Emethy warned, her voice steady despite the adrenaline coursing through her veins.

The creature snarled; its gaze locked on Emethy. For a moment, it seemed ready to lunge—but then it hesitated, its eyes flicking to the faint glow of her birthmark beneath her sleeve. The tension in its stance wavered, and it took a step back, its growl softening.

Alaric stepped forward cautiously, his hand on the hilt of his sword. "What is it doing?" he murmured.

"I don't know," Emethy replied, her brow furrowing. The creature's behavior was strange, almost as if it recognized her.

Without warning, the wolf-like beast turned and disappeared into the fog, leaving them in stunned silence.

Lyra was the first to speak. "That was no ordinary animal."

Emethy nodded, her grip on her dagger loosening. "We need to get back to the village."

Alaric's eyes lingered on her, a flicker of curiosity and concern crossing his face. "Lead the way."

Back in the village, Aunt Marella was tending to a group of villagers who had come seeking Emethy's healing touch. The air in the cozy cottage was filled with the aroma of herbs and the soft murmur of conversation. Marella's warm laughter rang out as she shared a joke with one of the farmers.

When Emethy and Alaric entered, Marella's eyes lit up. "Ah, there you are! And you've brought company."

Alaric smiled politely, but it was Darion, standing in the corner with his arms crossed, who caught Emethy's attention. His piercing blue eyes flicked to her; his expression unreadable.

"Emethy, you're late," Marella teased. "These folks have been waiting for you."

Emethy set down her satchel and began tending to the villagers, her hands deftly preparing salves and poultices. Alaric, ever the charmer, joined in, offering to help with simple tasks. The villagers were delighted, laughing at his awkward attempts to crush herbs under Marella's sharp instructions.

At one point, a child tugged at Darion's cloak. "Why don't you help too, mister?"

Darion blinked, caught off guard. "I'm not much for herbs," he said gruffly, but the child's earnest eyes made him relent. He crouched down to hand Emethy a bundle of bandages, their hands brushing briefly. Emethy glanced at him, surprised by the fleeting softness in his gaze before he quickly looked away.

As the evening wore on, the tension in the room eased. Laughter and warmth filled the space, and even Lyra seemed less brooding as she hovered near the rafters, watching the scene unfold.

When the last of the villagers had left, Marella shooed everyone out of the kitchen. "Go, rest. You've all done enough for today."

Alaric leaned against the doorway, a mischievous glint in his eye. "I didn't realize healing could be so lively."

Emethy rolled her eyes, but a small smile tugged at her lips. "You've got a lot to learn, city boy."

As they prepared to leave, Darion lingered near the door. His usual stoic demeanor softened just enough for Emethy to notice. "You should be careful in the forest," he said quietly. "There's more out there than just wolves."

Emethy tilted her head, studying him. "I'll keep that in mind."

Unbeknownst to her, Darion's concern was more than just duty. But like everything else he felt, he kept it buried deep, hidden behind a wall of indifference.

As the night settled over Thistledown, Emethy couldn't shake the feeling that her life was on the cusp of something monumental. And for the first time in a long while, she allowed herself to wonder what it might be.

Chapter 18

Whispers of a New Dawn

&

The Oracle's Truth

Morning broke with golden light filtering through the thick canopy of Thistledown's towering trees. Emethy's days had taken on an unexpected rhythm, one she hadn't anticipated when Alaric's arrival upended her routine. The villagers, charmed by his amicable demeanor, had begun treating him as one of their own. Yet, for Emethy, the days were a confusing blend of warmth and unease.

Lyra's jealousy only added to the tension. Her usual playful curiosity had soured into pointed silence whenever Alaric was nearby. She floated beside Emethy as she prepared herbs in the garden that morning, her arms crossed and lips pursed.

"You know he's hiding something," Lyra said, breaking the silence.

Emethy snipped a sprig of thyme, her gaze fixed on her task. "You've said that already."

Lyra's glow dimmed slightly, a sign of her growing frustration. "And yet you won't listen. When this falls apart, don't say I didn't warn you."

Before Emethy could reply, Aunt Marella's cheerful voice called out from the cottage. "Emethy, my dear! The Bakers have brought their little one. He's got another cough."

Emethy wiped her hands on her apron and made her way inside, Lyra trailing behind her like a disapproving shadow. The small cottage was bustling with life. Villagers were gathered in the main room, waiting for remedies or advice. Alaric stood near the hearth, laughing with Aunt Marella as she recounted some humorous tale. Darion, ever the stoic observer, leaned against the far wall, his sharp eyes taking in every detail of the room.

The Bakers, a kind couple with a mischievous toddler, approached Emethy. The boy's cheeks were flushed, and he clung to his mother's skirts.

"Emethy," the mother began, "he's been coughing all night. We didn't know what else to do."

Emethy knelt to the boy's level, offering him a gentle smile. "Let's see what we can do, little one."

As she worked, Alaric stepped forward, watching her with quiet admiration. "You've got a way with people," he said when she'd finished giving instructions to the Bakers.

Emethy glanced at him; her expression guarded. "It's just practice."

"No," Alaric said, his voice soft but firm. "It's more than that."

Their eyes met briefly before Darion's voice cut through the moment. "You should check the stores of feverfew, Emethy. We've been using a lot of it lately."

Emethy straightened, nodding. "I'll do that." She turned to Marella, who shooed her with a wave of her hand.

As the day wore on, the cottage buzzed with activity. Marella's sharp wit had the villagers laughing, even Alaric couldn't help but chuckle. At one point, a farmer's wife spilled a basket of apples, and Alaric's fumbling attempts to help retrieve them left the room in fits of laughter.

"City boy," Darion muttered under his breath, earning a smirk from Emethy.

Even Lyra seemed to begrudgingly enjoy the lively atmosphere, though her expression soured every time Alaric and Emethy exchanged words. When the last villager had been seen to, and the cottage grew quiet, Marella leaned back in her chair, fanning herself with a handkerchief.

"That Alaric is quite the helper," she said with a knowing look at Emethy.

Emethy rolled her eyes. "Don't start, Aunt Marella."

"I'm just saying, dear. He's easy on the eyes and good with his hands. What more could you want?"

Lyra let out a derisive snort, her ghostly form flickering. "A soul, perhaps."

Emethy fought back a laugh as she gathered her things. "I'll be in the garden."

Outside, the sun was beginning to dip below the horizon, casting the village in warm, golden light. Emethy busied herself checking the herb stocks, her mind drifting. She thought of Alaric, of Darion's quiet intensity, and of Lyra's warnings. The threads of her life felt tangled, pulling her in different directions.

As she worked, Alaric appeared, his approach heralded by the crunch of gravel underfoot. "Need a hand?" he asked.

Emethy hesitated, then nodded. Together they worked in silence, the air between them heavy with unspoken words. Finally, Alaric broke the silence.

"You're remarkable, you know that?" he said, his voice low.

Emethy looked at him, her brow furrowed. "What do you mean?"

"The way you care for people. The way you handle everything thrown at you. It's... inspiring."

Emethy's cheeks warmed, and she turned back to her task. "You don't know me well enough to say that."

"Maybe not," Alaric admitted. "But I'd like to."

Before Emethy could respond, a shadow passed over the garden. She looked up to see Darion standing at the edge of the path, his expression unreadable.

"Marella's calling for you," he said to Emethy, his tone neutral.

"I'll be right there," she replied.

Darion lingered for a moment, his eyes flicking between Emethy and Alaric, before he turned and walked away. Alaric watched him go, a small frown tugging at his lips.

"He doesn't like me much, does he?"

Emethy shook her head. "Darion doesn't like anyone."

Alaric chuckled, but the sound lacked its usual warmth. "Fair enough."

As the last rays of sunlight faded, Emethy found herself once again caught between conflicting emotions. Lyra's warnings echoed in her mind, but Alaric's sincerity chipped away at her defenses. And then there was

Darion, whose silent presence felt as steady and unyielding as the earth itself.

Unseen by any of them, a pair of eyes watched from the shadows, their intent shrouded in mystery. Later that night, Emethy woke up from a nightmare she kept to herself and stepped outside for fresh air.

The sun bathed the village of Thistledown in warm, golden hues as the weekly flea market bustled with energy. Merchants shouted to advertise their goods, children darted between stalls, and the mingling scents of roasted nuts and freshly baked bread filled the air. Emethy walked amidst the crowd, her senses tingling with unease. Lyra flitted silently by her side, her presence a whisper no one else could feel.

"You look like you've seen a ghost," a jovial merchant commented as she browsed his wares. Emethy managed a weak smile, then moved on.

As she turned a corner, her eyes fell upon a small, tattered tent at the edge of the market. Its dark fabric swayed in the breeze, and a wooden sign etched with intricate symbols hung above the entrance. Something about it felt out of place, as though it didn't belong in the lively chaos of the market. Lyra hovered uneasily beside her.

"Don't go in there," Lyra said, her voice sharp. But Emethy's curiosity was already piqued. Ignoring the spirit's warning, she stepped closer.

The air inside the tent was heavy with the scent of burning herbs. Candles flickered, casting long shadows across a table draped in crimson cloth. Behind it sat an elderly woman, her eyes clouded with a milky haze. Yet when she spoke, her voice was unnervingly clear.

"You've been walking a dangerous path, child," the woman said without preamble. "Come, sit."

Emethy hesitated before lowering herself onto the stool opposite the woman. Lyra remained just outside the tent, her presence a nervous hum in Emethy's mind.

The fortune teller's gnarled hands moved deftly across the table, flipping cards marked with strange symbols. Her gaze seemed to pierce through Emethy.

"Your guardian is death," the woman said at last. "You will meet her soon."

Emethy's breath hitched. "What do you mean?"

The woman leaned closer, her expression unreadable. "You'll find out when the time is right. But beware... not all who walk beside you are as they seem."

Before Emethy could press further, the woman abruptly stood, her movements swift for someone of her apparent age. "Leave now," she commanded. "Your questions will only find answers in time."

Emethy stumbled out of the tent, her heart racing. Lyra was waiting for her, her ethereal face clouded with worry.

"You shouldn't have gone in there," Lyra whispered. "That woman... she knows things best left forgotten."

But Emethy's mind was already racing, piecing together fragments of the cryptic warning. Who was her guardian? And why would she meet her soon?

As the two of them made their way back to Marella's cottage, the market's vibrant colors seemed muted. The fortune teller's words echoed in Emethy's mind, mingling with her memories of the shadow she had seen with Marella.

By the time they reached the edge of the forest, the sun had begun its descent, casting long shadows across the path. Lyra hovered close to Emethy, her silence a rare and disconcerting thing.

"Do you think it means something?" Emethy finally asked, breaking the uneasy quiet.

Lyra didn't respond immediately. When she did, her voice was barely audible. "It always does."

Lyra floated beside Elara; her voice full of concern. "Do you think Alden might be lying? Or is he playing tricks on you?" Her words hung in the air, the doubt in her tone sharp.

Elara's fists clenched, her patience wearing thin. "Stop asking so many questions, Lyra!" she snapped, her voice trembling with anger. "I don't need you!"

The words stung more than Elara intended, but the frustration was overwhelming. Lyra fell silent, her light flickering as if wounded by the harshness of the moment.

With a flick of her translucent form, Lyra drifted away, the space between them growing as she shrugged off Elara's words, disappearing into the shadows.

Chapter 19

The Knife Behind the Smile

Moonlight poured over the quiet village of Thistledown, casting silver shadows across the landscape. Inside Marella's cottage, the faint crackle of the dying hearth was the only sound. Emethy stirred restlessly in her bed, trapped in the throes of a nightmare that had haunted her for years. A dark forest, shadows that whispered her name, and a figure she could never quite see. She awoke with a gasp, her skin damp with sweat.

She sat up, brushing tangled hair from her face. The air inside felt suffocating, and she quietly slipped outside, careful not to wake Marella. The cool night breeze kissed her cheeks as she stepped into the open, her bare feet brushing against the dewy grass. The forest loomed ahead, silent and enigmatic, as if it held secrets she was not yet meant to uncover.

She exhaled deeply, her heart still racing from the nightmare. As she wandered toward the edge of the cottage grounds, a voice startled her.

"Can't sleep?"

Emethy turned to find Darion leaning against a tree, his arms crossed. His silhouette was imposing in the moonlight, his dark eyes glinting with an unreadable expression. His tone was curt, bordering on dismissive, yet his gaze lingered on her a moment longer than necessary.

"What are you doing here?" she asked, recovering from her surprise. Her voice was sharper than intended.

"Guard duty," he replied, shrugging as if it were obvious. "The prince likes knowing his trusted men are close by."

Emethy rolled her eyes. "Of course." She turned away, unwilling to engage further. Yet she could feel his eyes on her, as if he were trying to decipher something he couldn't quite grasp.

"You shouldn't wander around at night," he added, his tone softening slightly. "It's dangerous."

Emethy didn't respond, stepping further into the open air. The tension between them lingered, an unspoken current she chose to ignore. She moved toward the edge of the cottage, her attention caught by a flicker of movement near the treeline. Her breath hitched as she recognized the figure of her aunt Marella.

Marella was meeting someone—a shadowy figure whose features were obscured in the moonless night. The two spoke in hushed tones, their body language tense. Emethy's heart pounded as she crouched behind a low shrub, her mind racing with questions. Who was this person? And why would her aunt meet them in secret?

She glanced back, relieved to find Darion's attention elsewhere. He had turned away, seemingly disinterested, though his posture remained alert. Emethy waited until the shadow disappeared into the woods and Marella returned to the cottage before retreating herself. She slipped back inside, her movements careful and silent, her mind a storm of unanswered questions.

The next morning, sunlight streamed through the cottage windows, banishing the night's shadows but not Emethy's lingering unease. She busied herself with chores, her mind replaying the midnight encounter.

Marella was her only family, her anchor in a world of uncertainties. The thought that she might be hiding something felt like a betrayal.

Darion, as always, remained close to the prince but had found his way to the cottage's doorstep. He leaned against the frame, watching the morning bustle with a detached air. Villagers came and went, bringing small gifts and seeking Marella's wisdom or Emethy's healing touch. Among them, Darion stood apart, a silent observer.

As Emethy carried a basket of herbs outside, she accidentally brushed past him. "Excuse me," she said curtly, refusing to meet his gaze.

"Careful," he said, his tone laced with sarcasm. "Wouldn't want you to trip."

She shot him a glare but said nothing, determined not to give him the satisfaction of a reaction. Yet, as she walked away, she could feel his eyes on her again, a quiet intensity that sent a shiver down her spine.

Darion watched her go, his expression unreadable. She was unlike anyone he had encountered—sharp-tongued, fiercely independent, and entirely uninterested in his presence. It irritated him. And yet, he couldn't help but admire the way she carried herself, the quiet strength she seemed unaware she possessed.

"Darion!" The prince's voice called from a distance, breaking his thoughts. He straightened immediately, his loyalty pulling him away. But as he followed the prince, his mind lingered on Emethy, much to his own frustration.

That evening, as the sun dipped below the horizon, Emethy sat on the cottage steps, her thoughts heavy. Lyra hovered beside her, silent for once. The events of the night before and the tension of the day weighed on her. She glanced toward the forest, the shadows deepening as twilight gave way to night. Somewhere out there, answers awaited her. But for now, they remained just out of reach.

The moon was high, casting an ethereal glow over Thistledown. The village was quieter than usual, the air thick with the scent of pine and wildflowers. Emethy had spent the evening tending to a sick child in the village and was now making her way back to her cottage.

The faint hum of cicadas filled the silence as she walked under the canopy of trees.

As she neared the clearing by the stream, a familiar voice stopped her in her tracks.

"Emethy."

She turned to see Alaric, standing near the water's edge. The prince's regal demeanor was softened by the gentle light of the moon, and he held a single white flower in his hand. He smiled at her, a disarming expression that tugged at something deep within her.

"What are you doing out here?" she asked, her voice tinged with suspicion.

"I couldn't sleep," Alaric admitted, stepping closer. "And I thought I might find you here."

Emethy frowned. "It's late. You should be resting."

"Perhaps," he said, his tone light. "But I find it hard to rest when my thoughts are elsewhere."

Her eyes narrowed slightly, but she said nothing. Alaric gestured toward the stream, where he had set up a small arrangement. A blanket was spread on the grass, surrounded by glowing fireflies and small enchanted lights that hovered in the air, casting a warm, golden glow. The scene was undeniably romantic, but something about it felt rehearsed, calculated.

"I wanted to show you something," Alaric said, extending his hand to her.

She hesitated before taking it, allowing him to lead her to the blanket. As they sat, Alaric began to speak of his travels, weaving tales of distant lands and forgotten kingdoms. His voice was smooth, enchanting, and for a moment, Emethy found herself drawn in.

But then, his tone shifted. "You're special, Emethy," he said, his eyes locking with hers. "More than you realize."

She stiffened. "What do you mean?"

Alaric reached out, brushing a strand of hair from her face. "I've seen many people in my life, but none like you. There's a strength in you, a light. It's... captivating." His hand lingered for a moment, and his gaze softened as he leaned in slightly, his intent clear.

Emethy stiffened, her instincts screaming at her to move, but her body seemed frozen. "Alaric," she began, her voice barely above a whisper, but before she could continue, he murmured a soft incantation under his breath. The words, foreign and lyrical, wrapped around her like an invisible thread.

A strange warmth spread through her chest, her limbs growing impossibly heavy. Her vision blurred as a faint dizziness overtook her.

"What... are you doing?" she managed to whisper, confusion and fear mingling in her voice.

"Shh," Alaric soothed, his arms steadying her as her knees buckled. "It's nothing to be afraid of. Just rest."

Emethy pulled back slightly, her instincts warning her of something amiss. "Alaric, I—"

The world tilted, and she found herself cradled in his arms. Panic flickered through her half-conscious mind as she tried to fight the enchantment, but her body refused to respond.

"Darion," Alaric called, his voice firm.

From the shadows, Darion emerged, his expression unreadable. He moved to Alaric's side, his sharp eyes flicking to Emethy, who struggled weakly in the prince's grasp.

"Take her," Alaric ordered. "We need to leave before anyone notices."

Darion hesitated for a fraction of a second before obeying. He carefully took Emethy from Alaric, his arms steady and warm despite his usual aloofness. As he held her, a pang of something unfamiliar stirred in his chest.

Emethy's eyes fluttered open briefly, her gaze meeting his. "You don't... have to," she murmured, her voice faint but filled with quiet desperation.

Darion's jaw tightened, but he said nothing. Instead, he shifted her weight and began walking, following Alaric's lead. The prince walked ahead, his expression one of satisfaction, while Darion's steps were slower, more measured. He could feel Emethy's fragile trust slipping away with every step he took, and it twisted something deep inside him.

As they disappeared into the night, the village remained blissfully unaware of the storm brewing just beyond the trees.

The morning sun rose over Thistledown, casting golden rays through the dense forest. The village was bustling with its usual activity, but Aunt Marella's cottage stood eerily quiet. Marella moved about the kitchen, her brow furrowed in concern. Emethy often wandered, but this time felt different. She hadn't returned all night, and Lyra was unusually restless, darting from window to door with a frantic energy.

"She does this sometimes, Marella," Marella muttered to herself, trying to calm her nerves. But her words held no conviction. Something felt off.

Outside, Lyra floated anxiously, her form shimmering faintly. She could sense Emethy's presence but felt it growing faint, distant. Determined, Lyra resolved to find her. The little spirit darted into the forest, her glow dimmed as she moved swiftly, her whispers of worry carried by the wind.

Meanwhile, Alaric and Darion rode steadily through the dense woods, a small retinue following them at a distance. Emethy, bound and gagged, lay in a makeshift carriage. She was only half-conscious, the remnants of Alaric's spell keeping her disoriented. Her wrists were tied with enchanted bindings, glowing faintly with runes that suppressed her strength.

The prince rode beside the carriage, a smug smile playing on his lips. "She's more stubborn than I anticipated," he remarked to Darion, who rode silently beside him.

Darion didn't respond, his face a mask of indifference. His grip on the reins was tight, but his sharp eyes flicked to the carriage now and then. Inside, Emethy stirred, her movements sluggish but defiant.

Alaric leaned closer to the carriage, speaking loud enough for Emethy to hear. "You see, my dear healer, this isn't personal. Well, not entirely. You're a means to an end. My father..." His tone darkened, his expression hardening. "He was humiliated, betrayed by those who should have knelt before him. They took everything from him. And you, Emethy, with your precious powers and that mark—you're going to help me restore what was lost."

Emethy glared at him, her eyes blazing even in her weakened state. "You're no better than your father," she hissed, her voice hoarse. "And you'll meet the same fate."

Alaric chuckled, shaking his head. "You've got spirit. I'll give you that. But spirit won't save you."

Darion's jaw tightened, but he remained silent, his gaze fixed ahead. As the group traveled, the tension between the three of them grew. Emethy, despite her weakened state, began to hurl defiant remarks at Darion whenever he came close to check on her.

"Following him like a loyal dog, aren't you?" she snapped one evening as Darion handed her a flask of water. "No thoughts of your own?"

Darion's expression didn't waver. "Orders are orders," he replied curtly, stepping back without meeting her eyes.

Emethy scoffed. "Coward."

Darion turned away, his steps measured, but his hands clenched at his sides. His silence only fueled Emethy's frustration, and she continued to needle him whenever she could.

But despite his aloof demeanor, Darion's actions spoke louder than his words. He ensured Emethy was fed, tended to her bindings with care, and adjusted her cloak to keep her warm at night. He never lingered, never offered explanations, but his subtle acts of kindness didn't go unnoticed by Emethy, even if she refused to acknowledge them aloud.

Back in Thistledown, Lyra's search led her to the outskirts of the forest, where she caught a faint trace of Emethy's energy. The little spirit pressed on, her worry mounting. She could sense danger, a looming shadow that seemed to grow stronger the closer she got to Emethy's trail.

Lyra's whispers reached the ears of the wind spirits, who carried her plea through the trees. The forest seemed to come alive, its rustling leaves and creaking branches echoing her desperation.

As night fell, the group set up camp in a clearing. Alaric retired early, leaving Darion to keep watch. Emethy sat by the fire, her wrists still bound, her gaze sharp as she studied Darion.

"You're not like him," she said suddenly, her voice soft but firm.

Darion glanced at her, his expression unreadable. "You don't know me."

"I know enough," she replied. "You could've hurt me. You haven't."

Darion didn't respond, his eyes returning to the fire. The silence stretched between them, heavy with unspoken words. Emethy leaned back against a tree, her exhaustion finally overtaking her. But even as she drifted to sleep, her mind raced with thoughts of escape, of survival.

Darion's gaze lingered on her for a moment longer before he resumed his vigil, the weight of his choices pressing heavily on his shoulders.

And somewhere in the distance, Lyra drew closer, her determination unwavering.

Chapter 20

The Captive

&

The Crooked King

The towering gates of the royal palace loomed ahead, flanked by banners bearing the crest of Alaric's lineage. Emethy's heart pounded as the carriage passed through the grand entrance, its massive doors creaking open. She glanced at Alaric, his expression hard and unreadable, while Darion sat silent, his gaze fixed on the road ahead.

Once inside, Emethy was pulled out of the carriage, her legs still weak from the spell Alaric had cast. She stumbled slightly, but Alaric's hand caught her arm. His grip was firm but not harsh.

"You'll see soon enough why this is necessary," he said, his tone cold but tinged with an emotion Emethy couldn't place.

The palace was a masterpiece of stone and gold, its walls adorned with tapestries depicting ancient battles and victories. Servants hurried out of sight as Alaric led Emethy through the grand hallways.

Finally, they entered a dimly lit chamber. The room smelled of herbs and old parchment, with shelves lined with ancient books and scrolls. In the center of the room sat a man in a grand wheelchair, his face pale and sunken, his once-powerful frame reduced to frailty. A single guard stood behind him, watchful and stoic.

"This is my father," Alaric said, his voice softening ever so slightly.

Emethy's breath hitched. This was the man she had fought against, the ruler who had wrought terror across lands. But now, he was a shadow of his former self, his body broken, his power diminished.

The King's eyes met hers, sharp and calculating despite his weakened state. "So, this is the girl," he rasped, his voice like gravel.

"She's the key," Alaric replied. "When the full moon rises, everything will be as it should."

Emethy's head whipped toward Alaric. "What are you talking about?"

Alaric ignored her, stepping closer to his father. He knelt before him, the weight of his determination palpable. "I will restore what was lost. Your strength, your reign—it will all return."

The King placed a bony hand on Alaric's shoulder, his lips curling into a faint, cruel smile. "You've done well, my son."

Emethy's stomach churned. She tried to back away, but Darion stood behind her, blocking her path. His expression was unreadable, but she caught the slightest flicker of discomfort in his eyes.

Alaric turned to her. "You'll remain here until the full moon. Then, the spell will be complete."

"What spell?" Emethy demanded, her voice trembling with both fear and anger.

Alaric stepped closer, his face inches from hers. "A spell that will restore my father's power and ensure our legacy remains unbroken. You, Emethy, are the key to it all."

Emethy's blood ran cold. "You're insane if you think I'll help you."

"You don't have a choice," Alaric said with a smirk. "The full moon will draw the power from you whether you want it or not."

He gestured to Darion. "Take her to the tower. Make sure she's guarded."

Darion's jaw tightened, but he nodded. "As you command."

Emethy tried to resist as Darion led her away, but her strength was no match for his. He didn't speak, even as she hurled accusations and demands at him. When they reached the tower, he opened the door and motioned for her to enter.

"You don't have to do this," she said, her voice breaking.

Darion's eyes met hers for a fleeting moment, a flash of something unspoken passing between them. Then, he closed the door, the sound of the lock clicking echoing in the cold, stone room.

Alone, Emethy sank to the floor, her mind racing. The full moon was only days away, and she had no idea how to escape. The only thing she knew for certain was that she couldn't let Alaric succeed.

Outside her window, the moon hung in the night sky, its glow a reminder of the time slipping away. Emethy sat on the cold stone floor of her chamber, her knees drawn to her chest, the faint glow of moonlight creeping through the small, barred window. Her thoughts spiraled back to the time when everything seemed simpler—when Alaric was just the boy who smiled at her across the meadows of Thistledown. She ran her fingers over her birthmark, its glow muted now, as if reflecting her own diminishing hope.

"How could he have changed so much?" she thought, her voice a whisper in the silence. *"The boy I once cared for... The one who promised to protect me... How did he become this stranger?"*

Her mind replayed the memories of his laughter, his kindness, and the way he used to talk about justice and honor. Those words now felt hollow, drowned in the actions of a man consumed by ambition. She clenched her fists, anger rising to meet the sadness in her heart. *"I was a fool to believe in him."*

The sound of heavy footsteps echoed in the corridor, pulling her from her thoughts. The door creaked open, and Alaric entered, his presence filling the room with an oppressive weight. Behind him stood Darion, his face as stoic as ever.

Alaric glanced back at Darion. "Wait outside," he ordered, his tone sharp.

Darion hesitated for a fraction of a second, his eyes flickering to Emethy before he stepped back and closed the door.

Emethy rose to her feet, her chin held high despite the uncertainty curling in her stomach. "What do you want now, Alaric?" she asked, her voice steady but cold.

Alaric studied her, his gaze unreadable. "You used to call me 'Alaric' with warmth, Emethy. Do you remember that?"

She scoffed. "I used to know a man who deserved it. I don't know who you are anymore."

His jaw tightened, and he stepped closer, towering over her. "You think I've changed? Everything I've done is for my father, for our kingdom. You of all people should understand loyalty."

"Loyalty?" she snapped. "You talk about loyalty while you're using me against my will. That's not loyalty, Alaric—it's betrayal."

His face darkened, the tension in the room thickening. "Betrayal?" he repeated, his voice low and dangerous. "You think I enjoy this? Do you think I wanted to force your hand? You left me no choice, Emethy."

"No choice?" She stepped forward, her defiance blazing. "You had a choice, Alaric. You could have been the man you promised to be. But instead, you chose power over everything else."

Suddenly, the silence was shattered by a sharp *crack* that cut through the air like a whip, the sound of a slap echoing through the cold stone walls. His voice loudly

"You will not speak to me like that," Alaric hissed, his hand still trembling from the strike.

Outside the chamber, Darion froze. The sound hit him like a physical blow, and his fist clenched involuntarily at his side. His jaw tightened, muscles coiled with the tension of someone caught between obligation and something... else.

Inside the room, Emethy's world tilted. The sting of the slap seared across her cheek, burning like fire. For a brief moment, everything seemed to freeze—her skin, her thoughts, even the breath in her lungs. But then, as if the blow had unlocked something inside her, she stumbled backward. Her hands shot out instinctively to steady herself against the cold, stone wall, but her heart hammered in her chest, and her pride felt more bruised than her skin.

The echo of Alaric's hand against her face rang louder than anything else. Her cheek was on fire, but it was the searing insult that burned deeper, the sting of humiliation that crawled under her skin.

Emethy's eyes burned with fury as she raised her hand to strike Alaric, her patience finally snapping. But before her palm could meet his cheek, his fingers closed around her wrist in a vice-like grip. A smirk played on his lips, but his eyes held something deeper—control, calculation. A sudden wave of weakness washed over her, her strength draining like water slipping through her fingers. Her knees buckled slightly, and her vision blurred at the edges. "You still think you can defy me, Emethy?" Alaric murmured; his voice laced with the spell's power. She gritted her teeth, refusing to give in, even as her body betrayed her.

She refused to let him see her falter. Emethy straightened with all the dignity she could muster, clenching her jaw so tightly it almost hurt. The tears that had sprung to her eyes hovered dangerously at the edges, but she refused to let them fall. *Not here. Not for him.*

Her eyes, though shimmering with a quiet fury, locked with Alaric's, cold and unwavering. Her voice came out like ice, thick with disdain.

"You think a slap will break me, Alaric?" she spat, each word dripping with defiance.

Alaric's lips curled into a cruel smirk, satisfaction gleaming in his eyes, as though he relished every second of this torment. "You're already broken, Emethy," he said softly, his voice like a whispered promise of more pain. "You just don't know it yet."

"You don't understand what's at stake."

"I understand perfectly," she said, her voice steady despite the pain. "You're willing to destroy everything and everyone for your obsession with your father's approval. But it won't bring him peace, Alaric. And it won't bring you peace either."

Alaric grabbed Emethy's arm, his grip bruising. "You'll understand soon enough," he said, his voice dangerously soft. "When the full moon rises, everything will make sense."

She wrenched her arm free, glaring at him. "You're delusional if you think I'll ever forgive you for this."

Darion outside hearing Emethy not giving up. Every fiber of his being screamed to intervene, to stop the prince from pushing her further into submission. But his feet remained rooted to the spot, like a man held captive by his own indecision.

In that moment, Emethy's gaze flicked to the door, and for a fleeting second, it was as if she could feel Darion there, his presence pressing in, a silent observer.

With a deep, trembling breath, she steadied herself. Her mind was a whirlwind of emotions, but her will remained unshaken. She would not let Alaric—nor Darion—see her break.

She spoke again, quieter this time, her words carrying the weight of a promise. "You will regret this, Prince Alaric. I will make sure of it."

The prince's smirk faltered, but only for a moment. He stepped back, raising an eyebrow, his eyes dark with the thrill of the control he held. "We'll see, Emethy. We'll see."

Alaric's gaze hardened. He turned on his heel and stormed out, slamming the door behind him. Darion stepped aside, his eyes meeting Alaric's briefly. There was a flicker of something—uncertainty, perhaps—but Alaric brushed past him without a word.

As the sound of Alaric's footsteps faded, Darion remained by the door, his heart heavy. He didn't dare enter, didn't dare face the woman inside. For the first time in a long while, he questioned the path he had chosen.

Chapter 21

A Rescue or Escape?

Emethy sat alone in the dim chamber, her hands trembling as she held the faint bruises on her wrist, a cruel reminder of Alaric's betrayal. Her heart, once so filled with care and admiration for him, now felt hollow, as if the very fabric of her trust had been torn apart. She stared at the flickering candlelight, her mind spiraling.

"How could I have been so blind?" she whispered to herself, her voice barely audible. "The Alaric I knew—the one I once trusted with my life—he's gone. Or maybe he was never real."

Her thoughts swirled in anguish, replaying his words and the way his eyes burned with vengeful purpose. Tears welled up but refused to fall. Her pride wouldn't allow it.

A faint knock echoed against the heavy wooden door, breaking her reverie. The door creaked open, and Darion stepped in, his expression as unreadable as ever. He avoided her gaze, keeping his hand on the hilt of his sword, his posture stiff and unyielding.

"What do you want?" Emethy's voice was sharp, but her words faltered slightly.

Darion hesitated, his eyes flickering toward her bruised wrists before looking away again. "Are you hurt?" he asked, his voice low and even, as if masking something deeper.

"Why do you care?" she shot back. "You're just another pawn in his game. Orders, right?"

Darion's jaw tightened, but he didn't respond. The silence stretched between them like an unspoken challenge. Finally, he exhaled sharply, stepping closer.

"You don't know what you're talking about," he muttered. "I do what I have to."

Emethy scoffed, standing abruptly. "Oh, I understand perfectly. You're just as complicit as he is. Watching silently, following his every command, no matter how vile. That's who you are, isn't it?"

Her words cut deep, though Darion's face remained stoic. He looked at her then, his piercing blue eyes glinting with something she couldn't quite place—a flicker of guilt, perhaps, or maybe frustration.

Darion's piercing blue eyes locked on hers, filled with a rare intensity that made Emethy falter. "You think I wanted to watch him do that to you?" he said, his tone quiet but charged with emotion. "Do you think I had a choice?"

Emethy folded her arms tightly, her voice trembling with contained fury. "You had a choice. You could have stopped him. Instead, you just stood there. You might as well have been the one holding me down."

Darion flinched, the accusation hitting him harder than he expected. His lips parted as if to speak, but then he closed them, his jaw clenching. Turning abruptly, he stared out of the window into the inky blackness, his profile rigid.

"I didn't want this," he muttered, so low she barely heard. "But my choices don't matter, do they? Orders are orders."

The room fell into a tense silence, the air heavy with words unsaid. Finally, Darion spoke again, his voice rough with frustration. "Do you want to keep fighting me, or do you want to get out of here?"

"We don't have time for this," he said finally. "Do you want to get out of here or not?"

Emethy blinked, caught off guard by his sudden proposition. "What?"

Darion turned back to her, his voice dropping to a near whisper. "I can get you out. But we have to leave now."

For a moment, she stared at him, trying to read his intentions. "Why would you help me?" she asked, her tone laced with suspicion.

"Because I'm tired of being his pawn," he said simply. "Now, do you want to escape, or do you want to stay here and wait for whatever he has planned for you?"

Before Emethy could respond, a faint noise outside the chamber made them both freeze. Darion gestured for her to stay quiet, his hand moving to his sword. They listened intently as muffled footsteps echoed down the corridor.

Darion leaned in close, his voice barely audible. "We'll take the servants' passage. Stay behind me, and don't make a sound."

The moment they turned the corner, two guards appeared, their swords drawn. Darion pushed Emethy behind him instinctively, his hand gripping his sword hilt. "Stay back," he ordered, his voice calm yet commanding.

But Emethy stepped forward, determination gleaming in her eyes. "I can fight," she said firmly, pulling a slender blade from her belt.

Darion glanced at her, momentarily stunned. "You?" he started, but there was no time for more. The guards charged.

Darion met the first guard with a clash of steel, his movements swift and deliberate. Emethy sidestepped, engaging the second guard with surprising agility. Her blade moved with precision, deflecting strikes and countering with practiced ease.

Darion, mid-swing, caught sight of her out of the corner of his eye. Emethy ducked under a swing, her blade slicing through the guard's armor with a deft movement. Her speed and control were astonishing.

Within moments, the guards lay defeated, their bodies slumping to the ground. Emethy wiped her blade on the hem of her tunic, her breath steady despite the exertion.

Darion sheathed his sword, a slow smirk spreading across his face. "So you know how to swing a sword," he said, his tone laced with teasing amusement.

Emethystin shot him a glare, though there was a flicker of pride in her expression. "Surprised?"

Darion chuckled softly. "More impressed than surprised," he admitted, gesturing for her to follow. "Come on. We need to keep moving."

She gave a small nod, suppressing her emotions for now. Darion led the way, opening a concealed door at the back of the chamber. "Stay close," he muttered, his tone softer this time, and she followed him into the unknown.

The passage was dark and narrow, the air damp and cold. Darion moved swiftly but cautiously, his movements precise and calculated. Emethy followed closely, her breaths shallow. They reached a small courtyard, where the cool night air hit her face. For a brief moment, she felt a sliver of hope.

As they approached the edge of the palace grounds, Darion finally broke the silence. "We'll head into the woods. It'll be safer there."

Emethystin glanced at him, still wary. "And what then? You hand me over to someone else?"

Darion stopped, turning to face her fully. "Believe what you want," he said, his voice clipped. "But I'm getting you out of here. After that, you're on your own."

Emethystin stared at him, her emotions a tangle of anger, fear, and confusion. Finally, she nodded, and they slipped into the shadows of the forest, leaving the palace and its horrors behind.

The forest stretched endlessly before them, its ancient trees casting long shadows in the dim light of early dawn. The chill of the night clung to the air, and Emethystin tightened her cloak around her shoulders as she followed Darion, his silent figure moving ahead with purpose. The tension between them had not yet faded, but the quiet peace of the forest seemed to calm her thoughts.

They had traveled through the night, barely stopping to catch their breaths. Darion, as always, had been stoic, his focus fixed on the path ahead. Emethy, however, could feel the weight of everything pressing down on her. The memories of Alaric's betrayal, the pain of her captivity, and the uncertainty of what lay ahead all churned within her.

She finally broke the silence. "Darion," she said, her voice softer than she intended. "Where are we even going?"

He glanced back briefly, his piercing blue eyes unreadable. "Away," he replied simply, his voice low and even.

Emethy sighed, frustration bubbling beneath her calm façade. "That's not an answer. You can't just keep running without a plan. You know Alaric will follow us. He'll come for me."

Darion stopped abruptly, turning to face her. "Do you have a better idea?" he asked, his tone sharp. "Because from where I stand, staying anywhere near Thistledown is a death sentence for you. And I don't intend to die for someone who—"

He cut himself off, his jaw tightening. Emethystin crossed her arms, meeting his gaze with a defiance that surprised even herself. "Who what, Darion? Say it."

He exhaled heavily, running a hand through his hair. "Someone who doesn't even trust me," he muttered. "But fine. If you want a plan, here it is: We keep moving until we find a place where Alaric's reach doesn't extend."

"And where exactly is that?" she challenged, her voice rising slightly. "He's a prince. His reach extends farther than you think."

For a moment, neither of them spoke. The weight of her words hung in the air, and Darion's expression softened, though only slightly. Finally, Emethy spoke again, her tone quieter. "I don't have anywhere else to go. Thistledown isn't safe anymore, and even if it were, I can't go back. Not yet."

Darion studied her for a long moment, his blue eyes searching hers. "What are you asking me, Miss Emethystin?"

She hesitated, unsure of how to put her thoughts into words. Finally, she said, "If you're just running, then let me run with you. At least for now."

He raised an eyebrow, a faint flicker of amusement crossing his face. "You want to wander aimlessly with me? That doesn't sound like the Miss Emethystin I know."

Emethy's lips curved into a small, humorless smile. "Maybe I'm not the Emethystin you know anymore."

Darion's expression grew somber again, and he turned away, continuing down the path. "Fine," he said over his shoulder. "But don't expect me to make it easy for you."

Emethy fell into step behind him, her mind racing with questions. Despite his gruff demeanor, she couldn't shake the feeling that there was something deeper driving Darion—something he wasn't telling her. The way his shoulders stiffened whenever she mentioned

Alaric, the haunted look in his eyes when he thought she wasn't looking, all hinted at a pain he kept buried.

"Where are you really heading?" she asked after a long stretch of silence. "You say we're running, but it feels like you have a destination in mind."

Darion didn't answer immediately. When he finally spoke, his voice was quiet. "There's a place," he said. "Far from here. A safe place."

Emethy frowned. "Why do I feel like you're not telling me everything?"

He glanced back at her, his expression unreadable. "Because I'm not," he admitted. "And you'll just have to live with that."

Emethy opened her mouth to argue but stopped herself. Something about the way he spoke made her pause. There was a weight to his words, a pain that hinted at something far more personal than she could have guessed. For now, she decided, she would let it go.

They walked in silence, the tension between them slowly giving way to an uneasy truce. The forest around them grew denser, the shadows deeper, but Emethy felt a strange sense of comfort in the quiet. Whatever lay ahead, she would face it—with or without Darion's trust.

For now, they were bound by necessity, two wandering souls seeking refuge in a world that seemed determined to break them.

Chapter 22

The Scars We Carry

The full moon cast its silvery glow across the vast expanse of the land, bathing the palace in cold light. Alaric stood in the highest chamber of the east tower, his fingers gripping the edges of the ancient tome spread open before him. His frustration was palpable, his breaths shallow and erratic as he scanned the runes and incantations.

"Where is she?" he muttered, his voice laced with venomous determination. The spell he had been working on for weeks required her presence. Without Emethystin, his grand plan to restore his father's strength and his family's legacy would unravel.

"Emethystin," he whispered under his breath, closing his eyes. Magic hummed around him, the air charged with an unnatural energy. His hands began to glow faintly as he reached out, trying to sense her.

Meanwhile, deep in the woods, Darion and Emethystin had found shelter in a modest, abandoned cottage. The place was humble, with creaking wooden floors and the faint scent of damp moss. It wasn't much, but it was a reprieve from the chaos they'd left behind.

Emethy sat on the edge of the makeshift bed, her body heavy with exhaustion. The day's events had left her weary, and though she was grateful for the temporary haven, her mind was restless. She stared out of the small window at the moonlit forest, its beauty doing little to calm her nerves.

Darion leaned against the doorframe, his piercing blue eyes scanning the room before settling on her. "You should rest. We don't know how long we can stay here."

Emethystin nodded but didn't respond, the weight of unspoken fears pressing down on her chest. Finally, she lay down, the coarse blanket offering little comfort. As sleep began to claim her, she felt an odd, unsettling pull deep within her, as if something was trying to reach her.

In the tower, Alaric's spell work intensified. His voice echoed with ancient words, and a vision began to form in his mind—faint but unmistakable. He saw her, curled up in a dimly lit room, and beside her, a figure he recognized as Darion. Rage bubbled to the surface as he clenched his fists, the image fading as quickly as it appeared.

"So that's where you are," he hissed, a sinister smile curving his lips. "You can't hide from me forever, Emethy."

Emethy woke abruptly, her heart pounding. The room felt colder, the air heavier. She clutched her chest, trying to calm the erratic rhythm of her breathing. Something was wrong—terribly wrong. She looked around the dim cottage, her eyes adjusting to the darkness.

A faint glow caught her attention. She froze, realizing it was coming from her shoulder. The birthmark at the back of her shoulder—a secret she had guarded fiercely—was glowing faintly in the moonlight. Panic surged through her as she scrambled to cover it, grabbing a loose drape nearby.

Darion, hearing her sudden movements, was at her side in moments. "What's wrong?" he asked, his tone sharp with concern.

Emethy shook her head, keeping her back turned to him. "Nothing. I'm fine."

Darion's eyes narrowed, his tone shifting to a softer concern. "You don't look fine." His gaze momentarily caught the faint glow seeping through the fabric she clutched tightly around her shoulder before he abruptly turned away, respecting her space. "That light... does it have anything to do with the mark you're hiding?"

Emethy stiffened, her grip tightening on the drape. "It's none of your business," she snapped, her voice trembling.

Darion didn't press further but kept his distance, his back to her. "Are you hurt?" he asked after a pause, his tone softer now.

"No," she murmured, though she felt far from okay. "I... I just feel drained."

Darion nodded, still not looking at her. "Rest. I'll keep watch."

Emethy lay back down, her heart still racing. She couldn't shake the feeling that Alaric was close, that he was reaching for her through some unseen force. She closed her eyes, trying to will away the fear, but the glow of her birthmark continued to faintly illuminate the room.

Outside, the woods seemed to hold their breath, the silence almost oppressive. Somewhere in the distance, Alaric's determination grew stronger. He would wait for the next full moon, the pink moon, to execute his plans. And Emethy, though miles away, could feel the weight of his gaze even in her dreams.

The morning sunlight filtered through the dense canopy of trees, casting dappled shadows across the forest floor. The crisp air carried the scent of dew and earth, a quiet reminder that they were far from the chaos of the palace. Emethy stepped out of the cottage, her movements hesitant as if she were reluctant to face the world outside.

She spotted Darion a short distance away, seated on a fallen log. His back was to her, his posture relaxed but purposeful as he sharpened his blades. The rhythmic scrape of the whetstone against steel filled the quiet morning, steady and unyielding.

Emethy hesitated, her heart still heavy with embarrassment from the night before. The memory of her glowing birthmark and Darion's concerned gaze lingered in her mind, making her cheeks flush. She had avoided looking at him since then, unsure how to bridge the silence between them.

Darion glanced over his shoulder, sensing her presence. His piercing blue eyes softened when they met hers. "Good morning," he said, his tone casual but kind. "Sleep well?"

Emethystin nodded but didn't speak, wrapping her arms around herself as if to shield against the vulnerability she felt. She shuffled closer, her gaze fixed on the ground.

Darion set down the whetstone and leaned back slightly, his expression thoughtful. "You've been quiet since last night," he said, his voice gentle but probing. "Is it about what happened?"

Emethy's lips tightened into a thin line. She wanted to deny it, to shrug it off, but the words wouldn't come. Instead, she sank onto a nearby rock, her hands fidgeting in her lap. "I... I just feel exposed," she admitted finally, her voice barely above a whisper. "Like something that should have stayed hidden was laid bare."

Darion studied her for a moment before rolling up his left sleeve. The movement revealed a jagged scar that ran from his elbow to his wrist. "You're not the only one carrying marks," he said simply, turning his arm so she could see it clearly.

Emethy's eyes widened, her gaze shifting from his scar to his face. "What happened?" she asked softly.

Darion gave a faint, wry smile. "A mistake. One I paid for dearly. But it's a reminder, too. Every scar tells a story, Emethy. Some are visible, like this one. Others... well, they're buried deeper. But they're no less real."

Emethystin blinked, taken aback by the depth in his words. "And you... you don't feel ashamed of them?"

He shook his head, his expression thoughtful. "Shame is a heavy thing to carry. It'll weigh you down if you let it. Scars, though? They're proof that you survived. They're part of who you are."

Emethy's gaze fell to her hands, her fingers brushing against her shoulder where the birthmark lay hidden beneath her tunic. For the first time, she considered his words, letting them settle over her like a balm.

Darion's voice softened further, almost as if he could sense her inner turmoil. "Your birthmark… it's better than any scar I've ever seen. It's not a flaw, Emethy. It's a mark of something greater, something unique. You don't need to hide it."

A small, reluctant smile tugged at the corners of her lips. She glanced up at him, finding comfort in his steady gaze. "You have a way of making things sound less terrible than they are," she murmured.

He chuckled, a rare, genuine sound that warmed the cool morning air. "Well, someone has to. Otherwise, we'd all go mad."

For a moment, the tension between them eased, replaced by a quiet understanding. Darion picked up his blade and resumed sharpening it, the rhythmic scrape of the whetstone filling the silence once more. But this time, Emethy didn't feel the weight of embarrassment or fear.

Instead, she felt a small spark of hope—a fragile but promising step toward healing.

And as the sunlight broke through the trees, she allowed herself to sit quietly beside him, the scars they carried—visible and invisible—binding them in an unspoken truce.

Chapter 23

A Fractured Sanctuary

The cottage was cloaked in a fragile calm as the morning mist clung to the air, yet unease lingered within Emethy. Darion, ever practical, decided to go hunting, leaving her to recover her strength. "You need to eat," he had said, his tone firm but not unkind. "Rest here. I won't be long."

Emethy nodded, her energy still sapped from the mysterious force that seemed to tether her to Alaric's will. She watched him disappear into the trees, his blades at his side, a silent sentinel against the dangers lurking in the forest. The quiet of the cottage settled around her, heavy and oppressive. She tried to focus on her breathing, steadying herself as she fought the lingering sense of dread.

But the peace was short-lived.

The sound of hooves echoed faintly in the distance, growing louder with each passing moment. Emethy's pulse quickened as she stumbled to the window, her eyes narrowing at the sight of armored figures approaching through the trees. Palace guards. Her heart sank.

Before she could fully process their presence, the door burst open, and the guards stormed in. "By the King's orders, you are to come with us," one of them barked, his sword drawn.

Emethy reached for her own blade, her body moving on instinct despite her weakened state. "I won't go willingly," she spat, her voice trembling with defiance.

The first strike came quickly, forcing her to parry and sidestep in a desperate dance of survival. The clash of steel echoed in the small space, her movements sluggish but fueled by sheer determination. Emethy raised her hand, and with a surge of energy coursing through her veins, she struck the light. She managed to disarm one guard, but the effort left her breathless. Another closed in, his blade cutting dangerously close.

Emethy faltered, her knees buckling as her vision blurred. She barely registered the sound of footsteps pounding toward the cottage until a familiar figure appeared in the doorway.

Darion.

His eyes took in the chaotic scene in an instant, narrowing with fury. Without hesitation, he lunged at the nearest guard, his blade flashing in the dim light. The room erupted into chaos as Darion fought with the precision and ferocity of a seasoned warrior. Each strike was deliberate, each movement calculated. Within moments, the remaining guards lay defeated, their groans of pain the only sounds breaking the heavy silence.

Darion turned to Emethy, his expression a mixture of concern and barely restrained anger. She was on the floor, her sword slipping from her grasp as her body gave out. "Emethy," he said, his voice uncharacteristically soft as he knelt beside her. "Stay with me."

She blinked up at him, her vision swimming. For the first time, she saw something different in his eyes—a depth of emotion he usually kept hidden. It was worry, raw and unguarded.

"I'm fine," she murmured, though her voice was weak and unconvincing.

Darion didn't reply. He carefully lifted her into his arms, his grip firm but gentle. Outside, his horse waited, its reins tied to a nearby tree. He mounted swiftly, settling her in front of him. Her head lolled against his chest, and she muttered something incoherent, her strength waning.

"Just hold on," he said, his voice a low rumble against her ear. "We'll find a safe place."

Emethy's eyes fluttered open briefly, catching a glimpse of his face. The lines of tension around his mouth, the way his jaw was set with determination—it was a side of Darion she hadn't seen before. He wasn't just her protector now; he was something more.

As the horse galloped through the forest, the rhythm of its hooves a steady beat against the chaos they'd left behind, Emethy's consciousness faded. But even in her half-aware state, she couldn't help but feel the strength of the arms holding her and the steady heartbeat beneath her cheek.

And for a fleeting moment, she allowed herself to feel safe.

The forest was cloaked in the deep hues of twilight, its shadows stretching long and thin under the fading light. Emethy and Darion had journeyed far, their silence punctuated only by the occasional rustle of leaves and the distant calls of nocturnal creatures. Finally, they stopped beneath a towering oak tree, its branches forming a natural canopy that shielded them from the sky.

Darion set about gathering wood for a fire, his movements efficient and practiced. Within minutes, a small flame crackled to life, its warmth pushing back the chill of the evening. Emethy sat nearby, her back resting against the rough bark of the tree, her body heavy with exhaustion. She tried to close her eyes, hoping sleep would come quickly, but her thoughts were restless, darting from one worry to another.

Darion settled himself a short distance from her, his posture alert as he kept watch over their temporary refuge. The firelight danced across his sharp features, illuminating his piercing blue eyes, which scanned the darkness with a steady intensity.

As the hours passed and the fire burned low, Emethy drifted into a restless sleep. But it wasn't the peaceful reprieve she had hoped for. Her dreams were haunted by shadows, faces she couldn't recognize, and a growing sense of dread that tightened around her like a noose. She stirred, her breathing quickening as the nightmare deepened, until finally, she woke with a start, her body trembling.

Darion noticed immediately, his gaze snapping to her as she sat up, clutching her knees to her chest. For a moment, he hesitated, his usual stoicism warring with an unfamiliar urge to comfort her. "Nightmares?" he asked, his voice low but clear.

Emethy didn't respond, her eyes fixed on the dying embers of the fire. She hugged herself tighter, trying to steady her breathing. Darion shifted his position, leaning forward slightly. "You know," he said, his tone carefully neutral, "you don't have to carry it all inside. If you need to cry, just do it. No one's watching except the trees."

The awkwardness of his words made Emethy glance at him, her brows furrowing in surprise. "That's... strange advice," she muttered, her voice thick with emotion.

Darion shrugged, a faint smirk playing at the corner of his lips. "Maybe. But it works."

Emethy looked away, her throat tight. She hadn't cried in so long, not since leaving Thistledown. But now, the weight of everything—the fear, the pain, the uncertainty—was too much to bear. Without a sound, tears began to fall, streaming down her cheeks as she buried her face in her arms.

Darion watched her for a moment, his expression unreadable. Then, slowly, he moved closer, sliding to sit beside her. The gesture was tentative, almost hesitant, as if he weren't sure how it would be received. He didn't speak, didn't try to offer platitudes or empty reassurances. Instead, he tilted his shoulder toward her, a quiet invitation.

Emethy hesitated, but the rawness of her emotions overpowered her pride. She leaned into him, her head resting against his shoulder as she continued to sob silently. Darion remained still, his warmth steady and grounding. He glanced at her from the corner of his eye, noting the way her frame shook with suppressed grief.

After a while, her tears subsided, and the quiet of the forest wrapped around them once more. Darion tilted his head slightly, his voice soft but firm. "Feel better now?"

Emethy nodded faintly, her voice hoarse when she finally spoke. "I haven't... done that in a long time."

He gave a small, almost imperceptible nod. "Sometimes, you need to let it out. Carrying it all inside doesn't make you stronger—it just makes you heavier."

She straightened slightly, brushing at her tear-streaked cheeks with the back of her hand. Darion shifted back, giving her space, though the closeness they'd shared lingered in the air like an unspoken secret.

"You're not weak, Emethy," he continued, his tone turning more serious. "But you need to be careful. Don't trust anyone unless your intuition tells you to. And don't feel sorry for everyone just because you're a healer. Sometimes, being harsh is the only way to survive."

Emethy looked at him, her expression a mix of gratitude and curiosity. "You sound like you've lived through more than a few lessons yourself," she said quietly.

Darion's lips twitched into a faint smile. "Scars have a way of teaching you things," he replied, his gaze distant for a moment before returning to hers. "But they also remind you to keep going."

For the first time in what felt like forever, Emethy smiled—a small, hesitant curve of her lips that hinted at the resilience she still carried within. Darion noticed but didn't comment, instead turning his attention back to the forest. The fire crackled softly, its light casting flickering shadows around them as they sat in companionable silence, two wounded souls finding solace in each other's company.

Here's the revised version with Darion questioning Emethystin, starting from the next morning:

The first light of dawn filtered through the trees, casting dappled patterns on the forest floor. Emethystin stretched, feeling the ache in her limbs from their relentless journey. She turned to see Darion already awake, seated on a rock sharpening his blade, the rhythmic sound of stone on steel breaking the morning stillness.

"We can't keep wandering like this," Emethystin said, breaking the silence as she approached him. "I know a place where we can go. It's safe. And there are people there I trust."

Darion paused, his blade catching the morning light as he inspected its edge. "Do you really know it?" he asked, his tone skeptical. His sharp gaze met hers, as if measuring the certainty in her words.

Emethy folded her arms, slightly defensive. "Yes, I do. It's not far, and I'm sure we'll find some help there." Her voice softened. "I trust them. You'll see."

He held her gaze for a moment longer before shrugging and returning to his blade. "Fine. Lead the way. But if this 'safe place' turns out to be another disaster waiting to happen..." He didn't finish, letting the unspoken warning hang in the air.

Emethy rolled her eyes but said nothing, turning to pack her things. As she prepared to leave, she caught Darion smirking faintly—just enough to leave her wondering whether he was amused or simply preparing for the worst.

Chapter 24

The Workshop Reunion

The journey to Kellan's workshop was long but familiar to Emethy. The rugged path cut through dense thickets, where sunlight barely pierced through the canopy. Despite the weariness tugging at her limbs, Emethy's pace quickened as they neared the village outskirts. The faint, rhythmic clang of metal against metal echoed in the distance, mingling with the cheerful hum of a bustling marketplace.

Darion followed silently, his sharp eyes scanning their surroundings. He noted the shift in Emethy's demeanor—the guarded tension that usually cloaked her seemed to melt away, replaced by an energy he hadn't seen before. She seemed lighter, almost carefree, as if stepping into a piece of her past that still held warmth. Observing her joy, Darion thought, *"So this is what she's like when she lets her guard down."*

They reached a clearing where Kellan's workshop stood. The sturdy building was built of timber and stone, its wide-open front revealing a forge glowing with embers. Sparks flew as Kellan worked on a blade, his muscular frame moving with practiced precision. Nearby, Ploma stood sorting an array of herbs and vials on a wooden table, her bright eyes catching sight of Emethy first.

"Emethystin!" Ploma's voice rang out, filled with delight. She rushed forward, her arms outstretched.

Emethy's face broke into a rare, genuine smile as she embraced Ploma tightly. "Ploma! It's been too long."

Kellan looked up from his work, a grin spreading across his soot-streaked face. "Well, well, if it isn't the runaway healer. About time you showed up. I was beginning to think you'd forgotten us."

"As if I could," Emethy replied, her tone teasing. She turned to Darion, gesturing toward her friends. "Darion, meet Kellan and Ploma. They're family to me."

Darion inclined his head in greeting, his expression impassive. "Good to meet you."

Ploma's curiosity sparkled as she gave Darion a once-over. "And who might you be? He doesn't look like the type you usually travel with, Emethy."

Kellan smirked, leaning on the hilt of the blade he'd been working on. "He's got the brooding look down. Fits right in with you."

Emethy rolled her eyes, though a hint of color crept into her cheeks. "He's a... companion on this journey. It's a long story."

Ploma's expression softened. "Well, any friend of Emethy's is welcome here." She offered Darion a small smile. "Come, you both must be exhausted."

The group settled inside the workshop, where the warmth of the forge contrasted with the cool evening air. Ploma busied herself preparing tea while Kellan set aside his tools, wiping his hands on a cloth.

Emethy's gaze wandered over the familiar space, her chest tightening with a mix of nostalgia and relief. It had been months since she last stood here, yet everything felt the same—except her.

"So," Kellan began, breaking the silence, "what brings you back? Not that we're complaining, but you don't usually drop by without a reason."

Emethy hesitated, her fingers tracing the edge of her cup. "It's complicated. We're... searching for answers. And we need a safe place to rest."

Kellan's brows furrowed, but he nodded. "You've got it. Anything else you need, just say the word."

As the conversation turned to lighter topics, Emethy found herself laughing at Kellan's antics and Ploma's quick wit. For a moment, she felt a flicker of normalcy, as if the weight she carried had lifted ever so slightly. Darion observed quietly, his sharp gaze catching every detail—the way Emethy's laughter softened her features, the way Kellan and Ploma's presence seemed to ease her.

Later, as the evening settled into a comfortable quiet, Emethy's curiosity got the better of her. "So," she began, leaning forward with a sly grin, "are you two... together now?"

Kellan choked on his tea, while Ploma's eyes widened. "What?" they said in unison, exchanging a glance that made Emethy laugh. "Don't worry, I'm just happy to see you both so close. You deserve this kind of happiness."

Emethy chuckled, a playful glint in her eye. "Come on, it's a fair question. You've always been close, and I'd be happy for you."

Ploma flushed, her hands fiddling with the edge of her apron, then exchanged a shy glance with Kellan. "Well… we are. Together, I mean," Ploma admitted softly, her cheeks turning a deeper shade of pink.

Kellan smirked, though a hint of pride softened his expression. "Took us long enough, didn't it?"

Emethy clapped her hands together, beaming. "Finally! I couldn't be happier for you both. It's about time."

Ploma ducked her head, her shy smile growing as Emethy teased, "So, who made the first move? Kellan, I bet it was you. Ploma's too sweet to be bold like that."

Kellan chuckled, raising his hands in mock surrender. "Guilty as charged."

As laughter filled the room, Darion observed quietly from his seat, captivated by the way Emethy's joy lit up the space.

As the laughter faded, a somber note crept into the conversation. Ploma's expression grew pensive. "Have you... heard anything about Malentha?"

The question hung in the air, heavy and unspoken for too long. Emethy's smile faltered, and she shook her head. "No. She disappeared without a trace. I keep hoping I'll find some clue, but..."

Kellan's jaw tightened. "She always did like her secrets. But it's not like her to vanish completely. If anyone can find her, it's you."

Emethy nodded, though doubt gnawed at her resolve. As the fire crackled and the night deepened, the weight of Malentha's absence settled over them, a reminder of the unfinished chapters in their lives.

After the others retired for the night, Darion lingered near the forge, his thoughts a tangle of curiosity and reflection. He couldn't ignore the change in Emethy—

her laughter, her ease with these people. It was a side of her he hadn't known existed, and it intrigued him.

Kellan joined him, crossing his arms as he leaned against the wall. "She's something, isn't she?"

Darion glanced at him, his expression unreadable. "She's... different."

Kellan nodded, his gaze fixed on the fading embers. "She's been through hell, but she's still standing. That's more than most can say."

Darion didn't respond, his thoughts turning inward. As the night stretched on, he found himself wondering how much more he didn't know about Emethy—and how much he wanted to.

Chapter 25

The Festival & the Spell

As they approached the village, Kellan turned to Emethy and Darion with a wide grin. "You're just in time for the festival! The whole village has been preparing for weeks. It's one of the biggest events of the year."

Ploma nodded, her excitement palpable. "There's dancing, music, and a feast. Everyone in the village joins in. You'll love it, Emethy." She hesitated, then added with a teasing smile, "And maybe even Darion will crack a smile."

The village buzzed with excitement as the festival preparations began. Brightly colored banners fluttered in the breeze, lanterns were strung between rooftops, and the streets filled with the aroma of freshly baked bread and spiced meats. Children ran about, laughing as they helped carry small decorations, while villagers greeted one another with cheerful smiles.

Emethy couldn't help but feel a wave of warmth as she stepped into the lively scene. It reminded her of the festivals in Thistledown, though this one seemed brighter, fuller—as if untouched by the darker forces looming over her life.

Later, Ploma approached Emethy with a mischievous grin, holding out a folded dress of soft green fabric adorned with delicate embroidery. "You can't attend the festival in that," she said, nodding at Emethy's travel-worn clothes. "Here, try this on."

Emethy eyed the dress warily, her fingers brushing over the fabric. "I'm not sure this is… me," she murmured.

"Nonsense. It'll look perfect," Ploma insisted, practically shoving the dress into Emethy's hands. "Go on, I'll help."

Moments later, Emethy emerged from the workshop, tugging awkwardly at the neckline of the dress. "This is too tight," she muttered under her breath, trying to adjust it.

Darion, leaning casually against the doorframe, noticed her struggle and couldn't suppress a smirk. "Need some help?" he teased.

Emethy shot him a glare. "I'm fine."

"You look like you're wrestling with it," Darion said, stepping closer. His tone was light, but there was a flicker of amusement in his piercing blue eyes. "Here, let me."

Before Emethy could protest, he adjusted the ties at the back of the dress, loosening them slightly. "There. Better?"

She huffed, crossing her arms. "I didn't ask for your help."

"Could've fooled me," Darion replied, his smirk widening. "But you're welcome."

Ploma, watching from a few steps away, hid her smile behind her hand. "You two are impossible," she said, shaking her head.

Emethy glanced at herself, realizing the dress fit much better now. Reluctantly, she muttered, "Thank you."

Darion arched an eyebrow. "What was that? Didn't catch it."

"I said thank you," Emethy repeated, her cheeks flushing slightly. "Don't make me regret it."

Darion chuckled but said nothing more, following her as she joined the bustling preparations outside.

Kellan, ever the enthusiastic host, clapped Darion on the shoulder. "Come on, join in! This festival isn't just for watching, you know."

Darion frowned slightly, brushing Kellan's hand away. "I'm not exactly the festival type."

"Oh, nonsense," Ploma chimed in, her eyes twinkling. "Even the brooding ones need a little fun."

Emethy smirked at Darion's visible discomfort. "Maybe it'll do you some good to loosen up. Who knows? You might even enjoy yourself."

Darion shot her a skeptical look but followed as Kellan and Ploma led them deeper into the village square.

As the sun dipped below the horizon, the festival began in earnest. Musicians played lively tunes, and villagers took to the square, dancing in joyful abandon. Kellan and Ploma joined in with ease, Ploma's laughter ringing out as Kellan spun her around.

Emethy watched with a smile, feeling a rare sense of peace. But her attention quickly shifted when Kellan gestured toward Darion. "Your turn!" he called, grinning mischievously.

Darion stiffened. "No."

"Oh, come on," Ploma urged, stepping forward. "It's just a dance. No one's going to judge you."

Emethy joined in the teasing, her tone light. "Don't tell me the great Darion is afraid of a little music."

With a resigned sigh, Darion finally relented. "Fine. But don't expect me to be any good at this."

The villagers cheered as Darion stepped into the square. His movements were stiff and awkward at first, drawing good-natured laughter from the crowd. But as the music continued, he began to find his rhythm, surprising even himself. Emethy couldn't help but laugh, her eyes shining with delight.

Darion caught her gaze, and for a moment, the awkwardness of the dance faded. He thought, *This was a side of her he'd never seen before—a fleeting glimpse of the woman she might have been before all the burdens fell upon her.*

After the dance, the villagers gathered around long wooden tables laden with food. The air was filled with the hum of conversation, the clinking of cups, and the occasional burst of laughter. Emethy sat between Ploma and Darion, enjoying the warmth of the moment.

But as the evening wore on, she began to feel a familiar heaviness settle over her. Her limbs ached, and her head felt foggy. She pushed her plate away, her appetite gone.

Darion noticed her quietness, his sharp eyes narrowing in concern. "Emethy, are you all right?" he asked, his voice low so only she could hear.

"I'm fine," she said, though her voice lacked conviction.

Moments later, as she stood to leave the table, her knees buckled. Darion was at her side in an instant, catching her before she fell.

"She needs to rest," Ploma said urgently, rising to her feet. "Bring her back to the workshop."

Darion carried Emethy back to the workshop, his expression grim as he laid her gently on a cot. Ploma quickly gathered her herbs and supplies, motioning for Darion to wait outside.

"Let me work," Ploma said firmly. "I'll call you if I need help."

Darion hesitated but finally nodded, stepping outside and leaning against the wall, his arms crossed tightly. Inside, Ploma worked quickly, mixing salves and administering herbal remedies. But no matter what she tried, Emethy's condition didn't improve. Her breathing remained shallow, and her skin grew clammy.

Frustration etched itself onto Ploma's face as she placed a hand on Emethy's forehead, murmuring a prayer. It was then she noticed something unusual—a faint, unnatural glow emanating from Emethy's birthmark. Ploma's eyes widened in realization.

Darion stepped back inside just as Ploma straightened, her expression troubled. "It's not an illness," she said quietly. "It's a spell. Something dark is draining her."

Darion's jaw tightened. "Can you break it?"

Ploma shook her head. "This is beyond me. We'll need someone who knows more about magic. There might be someone in the outskirts of the village who can help, but it's a long shot."

Darion glanced at Emethy, his expression hardening with determination. "Then we'll take that shot. Whatever it takes."

As the night deepened, the festive joy of the village seemed like a distant memory. The fight to save Emethy had only just begun.

Chapter 26

The Ugly Creature

&

The Spirit World

The void was quiet and endless. Emethy drifted, her unconscious mind pulling her deeper into a realm she had never ventured before. The air shimmered with an eerie glow, and faint whispers surrounded her, their words unintelligible but heavy with sorrow.

Emethy looked around, her bare feet touching nothing yet feeling the coolness of something soft, like mist. Strange, ethereal lights floated around her, casting long shadows that seemed to flicker and move on their own. It was both beautiful and unsettling.

"Where am I?" she murmured, her voice echoing softly in the emptiness.

A figure emerged from the shadows, faint at first but growing clearer with each step. It was a woman, her translucent form shimmering with a faint blue light. Her features were sharp yet kind, her long hair flowing as if caught in a gentle breeze.

"You're in the place between," the spirit said, her voice calm but tinged with sadness. "The world where those like me linger."

Emethy took a cautious step forward. "Who are you?"

The spirit tilted her head, studying Emethy with piercing eyes. "Someone who knows much about you and your companion," she said cryptically. "You've brought Darion here, haven't you?"

Emethy's heart skipped a beat. "You know Darion?"

The spirit nodded, a sorrowful smile gracing her lips. "I do. More than he would ever admit."

Emethy hesitated before stepping closer, the spirit's aura both calming and unnerving. "If you know him, then why are you here? Why haven't you gone on?"

The spirit's gaze grew distant. "Because there are debts that bind me to this place. Debts that Darion now pays, though they were never truly mine."

"I don't understand," Emethy said softly. "What debts?"

The spirit sighed, her form flickering slightly as if the memory caused her pain. "When I was alive, I owed a debt to the king. Or so he claimed. It was a lie, created to justify his brother's actions. The truth was far darker."

Emethy's breath hitched. "What happened?"

The spirit's voice dropped, heavy with sorrow. "The king's brother desired something he could not have—me. When I refused, he used his power to brand me a traitor, claiming I owed a debt to the crown. He orchestrated my death to satisfy his lust and his pride, ensuring that Darion would never know the truth."

Emethy's fists clenched at her sides. "Darion is paying a debt that doesn't exist?"

The spirit nodded, her expression pained. "He believes his loyalty to the crown is his penance for failing to protect me. But he doesn't know… he never failed. The only ones who failed were the men who spun the lies."

Tears stung Emethy's eyes as she stared at the woman. "Who are you?" she whispered.

The spirit's lips curved into a bittersweet smile. "I am Aranel. Darion's sister."

Before Emethy could fully process the revelation, a familiar voice called out behind her. "Emethy! What are you doing here?"

Emethystin turned to see Lyra rushing toward her, the childlike spirit's face a mixture of worry and relief. Lyra's glow was brighter than usual, her tiny figure standing out against the muted tones of the spirit world.

"Lyra," Emethy breathed, her voice trembling. "I don't know how I got here. I was unconscious, and then..." She gestured at the surreal landscape around them.

Lyra's gaze shifted to Aranel, narrowing slightly. "Who is this?"

Aranel inclined her head, her translucent form shimmering faintly. "I exist here because my spirit age is not yet complete," she explained, her voice tinged with both sadness and acceptance. "When my time in this realm is fulfilled, I will move on to liberation. Until then, I remain bound to this place—not by choice, but by the natural order of things."

Emethy nodded slowly, her voice soft. "And in this time, you've seen things... things about Darion?"

Aranel's expression grew somber. "I have. Things he does not know and truths he may not yet be ready to face. But when the time comes, it will be you who must help him see.""

Lyra's eyes widened, and she looked back at Aranel. "If you're Darion's sister, then you must know how to help her get back."

Aranel nodded. "I do. But before she goes, she must remember what I've told her. Darion's burden is not his to carry. When the time comes, you must help him see that."

Emethy nodded, her heart heavy with the weight of Aranel's words. "I will."

The spirit's form began to flicker, her edges blurring as if she were being pulled away. "It is time for you to return," Aranel said, her voice fading. "And Emethy... tell him I'm proud of him."

Emethy reached out instinctively, but Aranel disappeared into the mist, leaving only silence behind. Lyra grabbed Emethy's hand, her small fingers surprisingly firm. "Come on. We need to go back.

The atmosphere in the workshop shifted abruptly, the warm glow of the forge replaced by an oppressive chill that sent shivers down Ploma's spine. Emethy lay unconscious on the cot, her breathing shallow and her face pale. Ploma's hands trembled as she adjusted the blanket over Emethy, a sense of unease creeping into her chest.

Then, a low, guttural growl echoed through the room. Ploma's head snapped up, her eyes widening in horror as the door creaked open, revealing a grotesque creature. It was hunched, with long, sinewy limbs and flesh that seemed to writhe and drip like tar. Its eyes glowed a sickly yellow, locking onto Emethy with a predatory hunger.

Ploma screamed, the sound piercing the quiet night. "Kellan! Darion! Get in here!"

The creature snarled, lurching forward as its gnarled claws reached for Emethy. Ploma stumbled backward, her voice trembling as she shouted again. "Hurry!"

Kellan and Darion burst into the room, their eyes darting between Ploma and the monstrous figure now looming over Emethy. For a split second, the two men exchanged a look—one of alarm and unspoken resolve.

"What in the world is that?" Kellan muttered, his voice low but edged with tension.

"Does it matter?" Darion shot back, drawing his sword in a fluid motion. "It's not leaving with her."

The creature let out an ear-splitting screech as Kellan lunged forward, his blade slicing through the air. The strike landed, cutting deep into the creature's side, but instead of retreating, it lashed out, its claws swiping dangerously close to Kellan's face. He ducked just in time, rolling to the side as Darion moved in, his sword glinting in the dim light.

Darion's movements were precise and deliberate, each strike aimed at the creature's joints and vulnerable spots. But the creature was fast, its unnatural agility making it difficult to land a fatal blow. It twisted and turned, its grotesque form defying logic as it evaded their attacks.

Kellan regrouped beside Darion, panting slightly. "This thing isn't going down easily."

"Then we keep hitting it until it does," Darion replied, his voice calm but steely.

As the two men launched another coordinated attack, the creature's focus remained on Emethy. It managed to grab her limp form, lifting her off the cot as if she weighed nothing. Ploma's panicked cries filled the room as she watched helplessly from the corner.

"No!" Kellan shouted, his sword slicing across the creature's arm. Black ichor sprayed from the wound, but the creature didn't release Emethy. Instead, it screeched again, its grip tightening around her.

Darion's jaw clenched as he moved in, his blade flashing. "Put her down," he growled, his voice low and menacing.

Just as the fight seemed to reach its breaking point, the room was plunged into darkness. The fire in the forge flickered and dimmed, and an unnatural stillness settled over the workshop. From the corner of the room, a shadow began to coalesce, its form taking shape until it resembled a tall, cloaked figure.

The creature froze, its yellow eyes widening in what could only be described as fear. The shadow moved with an eerie grace, extending a hand toward the creature. Without a word, the shadow unleashed a wave of dark energy that struck the creature, causing it to writhe and shriek. Its form began to disintegrate, black ichor dripping to the floor as it dissolved into nothingness.

The shadow lingered for a moment, its presence commanding and otherworldly. Ploma stared at it, her mind racing. "Is that... Malentha?" she whispered to herself, her voice barely audible.

Kellan, however, seemed unfazed. He lowered his sword and let out a slow breath. "No. It's not her."

The shadow turned slightly, as if acknowledging Kellan's words, before dissolving into the darkness, leaving the room in silence.

Darion rushed to Emethy's side, his sword still in hand. He knelt beside her, his expression a mixture of relief and lingering concern as he cradled her limp form. Darion's voice gentle yet firm as he brushed a stray lock from her face "Emeth, wake up… open your eyes for me,," he whispered, his tone laced with quiet urgency.

"Who was that?" he asked, his voice quiet but firm. Kellan sheathed his blade, his gaze steady. "It was death."

Ploma's eyes widened. "Death? Are you sure?"

Kellan nodded slowly. "I've seen her before. She's saved Emethy once already. And it seems she's done it again."

Darion's grip on Emethy tightened slightly as he processed Kellan's words. He looked down at her pale face, a flicker of something unspoken crossing his features. "Why?" he murmured, though no one had an answer.

Her eyes opened slowly, and the first thing she saw was Darion's face hovering above her, his piercing blue eyes watching her intently. His expression was a mix of relief and hesitation, as if he wasn't quite sure what to say.

Emethy's lips twitched into a weak smile as she found her voice, albeit faintly. "Darion…" she murmured, her voice soft and slightly hoarse. "Are you going to kiss me?"

Darion stiffened, a faint flush rising to his cheeks. He quickly looked away, his usual stoicism faltering for a moment. "That's not funny," he muttered, his tone gruff but laced with a hint of embarrassment.

Emethy managed a quiet laugh, though it took what little energy she had. "You're blushing," she teased lightly, her smile growing despite her exhaustion.

Darion's eyes snapped back to hers, his expression unreadable once more. "You're imagining things," he replied, his voice returning to its usual calm. But the way his gaze lingered on her for just a moment longer betrayed a flicker of something deeper.

Before Emethy could respond, Ploma stepped forward, breaking the tension. "She's awake," Ploma said, relief evident in her voice. "We should let her rest."

Darion carefully adjusted Emethy in his arms, standing to carry her back to the cot. He didn't say anything else, but as he laid her down, his hand lingered for a moment on her shoulder, a silent reassurance that she was safe.

As the workshop settled back into uneasy quiet, one thing was clear: the fight was far from over, and Emethy's connection to the spirit world was more dangerous than any of them had imagined.

Chapter 27

Silent Struggles

&

The Confession

The morning sunlight filtered through the windows of Kellan's workshop, casting a warm glow over the wooden table where everyone had gathered for breakfast. The smell of fresh bread and spiced tea filled the room, but the atmosphere was unusually tense.

Emethy sat quietly, her hands wrapped around a mug of tea. Her eyes were distant, unfocused, as if her mind were somewhere far away. Darion, sitting across from her, watched her carefully. The concern etched on his face was subtle but unmistakable.

"How are you feeling?" Darion asked, his voice steady but gentle.

Emethy didn't respond immediately, her gaze fixed on the steam rising from her mug. When she finally spoke, her tone was curt. "I'm fine. You don't have to keep asking."

The sudden sharpness in her words caught everyone off guard. Ploma glanced between them, her expression softening with worry, while Kellan raised an eyebrow but said nothing. Darion's brow furrowed, confusion flickering in his eyes. He opened his mouth to respond, but before he could, Kellan let out a light chuckle, breaking the tension.

"Ah, don't take it personally," Kellan said, shrugging. "She's probably just having a mood swing. Happens all the time, right, Ploma?" He gave Ploma a teasing nudge.

Ploma shot him a look but didn't argue. "She's just feeling low," Ploma said softly. "She'll be fine in some time."

Emethy pushed back her chair abruptly, standing without a word. The others watched as she moved toward the door, her steps brisk but unsteady. She paused for a moment before stepping outside, the door creaking shut behind her.

Darion glanced at Ploma, his confusion deepening. "What's going on with her? She was different yesterday. Now she's…" He trailed off, searching for the right words.

Ploma sighed, folding her hands in her lap. "This is just her way," she explained. "When something's weighing on her, she keeps it to herself. Going outside and sitting alone helps her think. It's how she copes."

"How long does she take to open up?" Darion asked, his tone more serious now.

Ploma hesitated, her eyes distant as she considered her words. "Sometimes it takes a few days. Sometimes longer. And sometimes, she never does. But we have to give her time. Some things are just hard to say."

Kellan nodded in agreement, leaning back in his chair. "You just have to hang on tighter, Darion. That's the thing about Emethy—she's strong, but even the strongest people need space to figure things out."

Darion leaned back, crossing his arms as he processed their words. His gaze flicked to the door Emethy had disappeared through, his thoughts swirling. He wasn't used to dealing with people like her, and the way she shifted between openness and withdrawal left him unsettled. But something about her—something he couldn't quite put into words—made him want to try.

Emethy sat on a large rock at the edge of the clearing, the cool breeze brushing against her face. She closed her eyes, letting the sounds of the forest wash over her—the rustling leaves, the distant chirping of birds. Her mind was a storm of thoughts, swirling around the words Aranel had spoken in the spirit world.

"Darion's burden is not his to carry."

The weight of the truth pressed heavily on her chest. How could she tell him? How could she look into his piercing blue eyes and shatter the foundation of what he believed about himself? The thought of it twisted her stomach into knots.

As she sat lost in thought, the sound of soft footsteps broke the silence. Emethy turned her head to see Ploma approaching, a cup of tea in her hands. Ploma didn't say anything at first, simply settling down beside Emethy and offering her the tea.

"Here. Thought you might need this," Ploma said quietly.

Emethy hesitated before taking the cup, the warmth of it grounding her slightly. "Thanks," she murmured.

Ploma sat with her in silence for a moment, staring out at the trees. "It's heavy, isn't it?" she said finally, her tone gentle. "Carrying it all. Feeling like you can't say it out loud."

Emethy's fingers tightened around the cup. "Even if I wanted to say it, I don't know how," she admitted.

Ploma turned to her, a soft smile on her face. "Start with the truth. Whatever it is, just let it out. Keeping it inside doesn't make it go away—it just makes it hurt more. For you and for him."

Emethy glanced at Ploma, her eyes searching. "I know something about Darion. Something I don't think he knows. But I don't know how to tell him. What if it makes things worse?"

Ploma rested a hand on Emethy's shoulder. "You'll know when the time is right. But don't wait too long.

Sometimes, sharing the weight is the only way to lighten it."

Emethy nodded slowly, her grip on the tea loosening. "I'll think about it."

"Good." Ploma stood, brushing off her hands. "Come back inside when you're ready."

After another moment of quiet reflection, Emethy rose to her feet and followed Ploma back into the workshop.

The room fell silent as Emethy walked in, her steps purposeful but hesitant. Darion's gaze met hers immediately, his expression unreadable.

Emethy stopped in front of him, taking a deep breath. "I'm sorry," she said softly, her voice barely above a whisper. "For snapping at you earlier. I… I didn't mean to."

Darion studied her for a moment before nodding. "It's fine. Take your time," he said simply, his voice calm and steady.

Emethy nodded in return, her lips pressing into a thin line. "Thanks," she murmured before moving to sit down at the table. The tension in the room eased slightly, though the unspoken weight of her thoughts lingered.

From across the table, Ploma caught Kellan's eye and gave a subtle nod. They all understood that Emethy's journey wasn't just physical—it was one of the heart and mind as well.

The clearing was quiet except for the sound of clashing swords as Emethy and Darion practiced. The sun filtered through the trees, dappling the ground with patches of golden light. Darion's strikes were precise and measured, his expression unreadable as he moved fluidly with his blade. Emethy, though not as skilled, held her ground, her movements driven by determination.

"You're still overextending," Darion said, his voice calm but firm. He stepped back, lowering his sword. "Focus on your footing."

Emethy sighed, brushing a strand of hair out of her face. "I'm trying. You make it look so easy."

"It's not," he replied, his tone softening slightly. "It just takes practice."

They resumed sparring, but Emethy's mind was elsewhere. Her grip on the sword tightened as she replayed Aranel's words in her head. The weight of the truth pressed heavily on her chest, and she knew she couldn't keep it to herself any longer.

When they paused again, Darion sheathed his sword and glanced at her. "You're distracted," he observed. "What's on your mind?"

Emethy hesitated, lowering her weapon. Her gaze dropped to the ground as she searched for the right words. "Darion," she began quietly, "I need to tell you something."

He tilted his head slightly, his piercing blue eyes narrowing. "What is it?"

Emethy took a deep breath, her fingers trembling slightly as she gripped the hilt of her sword. "When I was unconscious… after the creature attacked, I wasn't just dreaming. I was in the spirit world."

Darion's expression didn't change, but his posture stiffened slightly. He said nothing, waiting for her to continue.

"I met someone there," Emethy continued, her voice faltering. "She said she knew you. And she told me... she told me everything about what happened to her."

Darion's jaw tightened. "Who did you meet?"

Emethy swallowed hard, finally meeting his gaze. "Your sister. Aranel."

For a moment, the air seemed to still. Darion's expression remained unreadable, but his grip on the pommel of his sword tightened. "What did she say?" he asked, his voice low and carefully controlled.

Emethy stepped closer, her tone soft but steady. "She told me about the debt she was accused of, how it was all a lie created by the king's brother. She said you've been carrying guilt for something that was never your fault. Darion, she wanted you to know that you didn't fail her."

Darion's eyes darkened, his jaw clenching as he processed her words. He turned away, taking a few steps toward the edge of the clearing. "She told you that?" he asked, his voice barely above a whisper.

"Yes," Emethy said, her heart aching at the vulnerability he tried so hard to hide. "She said she was proud of you. She wanted you to let go of the guilt you've been carrying all these years."

Darion stood silent for a long moment, his back to her. When he finally spoke, his voice was strained. "I've carried this for so long, Emethy. I... I don't even know who I am without it."

Emethy stepped closer, her hand hovering near his arm but not quite touching him. "You're more than your past, Darion. Aranel saw that. And so do I."

He turned to look at her then, his blue eyes filled with an emotion she couldn't quite name. For the first time, his carefully constructed walls seemed to crack, revealing the weight he had been carrying for so long.

Emethy hesitated only for a moment before stepping forward and wrapping her arms around him in a gentle hug. Darion stiffened at first, unaccustomed to such gestures, but slowly relaxed, his arms hovering awkwardly at his sides.

The sound of someone clearing their throat broke the moment. Emethy quickly stepped back, her face flushing as she turned to see Kellan standing at the edge of the clearing, a smirk playing on his lips.

"Well, well," Kellan said, his tone dripping with amusement. "Are you two a thing now? Should I start planning a wedding?"

"It's not like that!" Emethy blurted, her voice higher than usual as she avoided Darion's gaze. "I... I just remembered something I need to do." She turned on her heel and hurried back toward the workshop, her cheeks burning.

Kellan watched her retreat, his grin widening. He turned to Darion, who was still standing where Emethy had left him, his expression unreadable. "You know, she doesn't trust people easily," Kellan said, his tone growing more serious. "Take good care of her, or I swear I'll kill you myself."

Darion gave him a sidelong glance, one corner of his mouth twitching upward. "Sometimes she acts like a child," he said dryly, "and other times like she owns the seven continents."

Kellan chuckled, clapping him on the shoulder. "That's Emethy for you. Just… don't screw it up, Darion."

Darion didn't respond, his gaze fixed in the direction Emethy had gone. But the hint of a smile lingered on his lips as he turned back to Kellan. "I'll do my best."

Chapter 28

The Bonfire Revelation

The sky above the clearing was painted with hues of deep indigo, scattered stars twinkling faintly against the darkness. The warmth of the bonfire crackled in the cool evening air, its golden light casting long, flickering shadows on the faces gathered around it. Ploma had prepared a soothing herbal tea, its earthy aroma blending with the smoky scent of burning wood. Emethy sat quietly, her hands wrapped around a warm cup, as Kellan and Darion settled into their places by the fire.

Ploma handed Darion a steaming cup before taking a seat next to Kellan. The atmosphere was calm but tinged with an undercurrent of tension, unspoken questions hanging in the air.

Kellan broke the silence first, his voice steady but thoughtful. "Emethy, there's something we need to talk about. Something that happened while you were... unconscious."

Emethy looked up from her tea, her eyes narrowing slightly. "What is it?"

Kellan exchanged a glance with Darion, who remained stoic but gave a slight nod. "A creature came for you," Kellan began, his tone grave. "It was… unlike anything I've ever seen. Grotesque, twisted, and powerful. It was clear it wasn't here by accident."

Emethy's grip on her cup tightened, her knuckles turning white. "Alaric sent it, didn't he?" she asked, her voice low but steady.

Kellan nodded. "I'm almost certain of it. That thing wasn't just trying to harm you—it was trying to take you. Darion and I fought it, but nothing we did seemed to work. It was… relentless."

Darion spoke then, his voice calm but edged with frustration. "Every strike felt meaningless. It was as if the creature absorbed our efforts and grew stronger. We couldn't stop it."

Kellan leaned forward, his gaze fixed on Emethy. "But then something happened. Out of nowhere, a shadow appeared. Darker than the night itself, it moved like it wasn't bound by the rules of this world. It went straight for the creature and destroyed it in seconds."

Emethy's heart pounded in her chest as she listened. She could feel the air grow heavier, the weight of their words settling over her. "A shadow?" she repeated softly, though she already knew the answer.

Kellan nodded again. "It was unlike anything I've seen. But there was something about it... something familiar. It didn't stay long. Once the creature was gone, it disappeared just as suddenly as it came."

Ploma, who had been quiet until now, added hesitantly, "When I saw it, I thought... I thought it might be Malentha. But Kellan disagreed."

Emethy lowered her cup, her fingers trembling slightly. "It wasn't Malentha," she said quietly, her voice carrying a certainty that silenced the group. She lifted her gaze to meet Kellan's. "It was Death."

The words hung in the air, heavy and undeniable. Kellan's jaw tightened, but he didn't argue. Ploma's eyes widened, her face pale in the firelight. Darion, for once, looked taken aback, his usual stoicism slipping for a fraction of a second.

"You've seen it before," Kellan said, his tone more a statement than a question.

Emethy nodded, her voice steady despite the storm of emotions swirling inside her. "Death has been following me for a long time. It's not the first time it's intervened. And I doubt it will be the last."

Darion's piercing blue eyes locked onto hers. "Why?" he asked simply, the single word carrying the weight of a dozen questions.

Emethy hesitated, her gaze dropping to the flames. "I don't know," she admitted. "But every time it appears, it's to protect me. I don't understand why, but I... I don't trust it."

The group fell into silence, each of them lost in their thoughts. The fire crackled softly, its light dancing on their faces. Finally, Kellan leaned back, letting out a slow breath. "Well," he said, his voice lighter but still thoughtful, "it seems like you've got quite the guardian watching over you."

Emethy offered a faint smile, though it didn't quite reach her eyes. "Guardian or not, Alaric won't stop. And neither can we."

Darion nodded in agreement, his expression hardening. "We'll be ready. Whatever comes next, we'll face it."

As the fire began to die down, the group sat in the quiet comfort of their shared resolve, knowing that the battles ahead would test them in ways they could not yet imagine.

The campfire crackled softly as night fell over the clearing, casting flickering shadows on the group. Emethy sat slightly apart from the others, her gaze fixed on the glowing embers as her thoughts swirled. Kellan and Ploma chatted idly about the day's chores, and Darion sat silently nearby, sharpening his blade with slow, deliberate movements. The rhythmic scrape of metal on stone was oddly comforting, but Emethy barely noticed.

She couldn't shake the weight of her thoughts. Death. The shadow that had intervened more than once. The being she had feared and loathed for so long now seemed inexplicably tied to her. Why was it saving her?

What did it want? Her fingers traced the edge of her birthmark absently, the faint glow she had seen in moments of danger haunting her memory.

Darion's voice broke through her reverie. "You've been staring at the fire for an hour. Planning to burn a hole through it?"

Emethy blinked, jolted back to the present. She turned to him, catching the faint smirk on his face. "No. Just thinking."

"That much is obvious," Darion said, his tone dry. He set the whetstone aside and leaned back, watching her. "What about?"

Emethy hesitated, her fingers tightening around the mug of tea in her lap. She wasn't ready to share everything. Not yet. "Nothing important," she said quickly, but the flicker in her eyes betrayed her words.

Darion arched an eyebrow, clearly unconvinced. "You're a terrible liar."

Before she could respond, Kellan's voice cut in. "Oh, leave her alone, Darion. Not everyone likes to spill their guts as easily as you sharpen a blade."

Darion shot him a glance. "I don't spill anything. Unlike you, apparently."

Kellan grinned, unbothered. "Still, it's nice to see you care. You're practically glued to her side these days."

Emethy groaned, the heat rising to her cheeks. "Kellan, don't start."

Ploma, ever the peacemaker, chuckled softly. "Come on, Kellan. Let them be. Not everyone enjoys your matchmaking attempts."

Kellan raised his hands in mock surrender. "Fine, fine. But it's not my fault you two act like an old married couple."

Emethy stood abruptly, brushing off her hands. "I need some air." Without another word, she stepped away from the group, heading toward the trees at the edge of the clearing.

Emethy sat alone at the edge of the clearing, her legs tucked beneath her, staring at the faint rays of sunlight breaking through the dense forest canopy. The world around her was alive with sound—birds chirping, the rustle of leaves, the distant hum of life—but her mind was elsewhere. The warmth of the sun on her skin did little to dispel the chill that lingered in her thoughts.

The shadow, the one they called Death, had saved her again. It was a mystery that both comforted and unsettled her. For as long as she could remember, Death had been something she despised, a force that had taken so much from her. Yet now, she couldn't deny the strange bond she felt with it.

Why is it protecting me? she thought, her fingers brushing absentmindedly over the birthmark on her shoulder. *What does it want from me?*

She had seen Death before—in the eyes of those she couldn't save, in the quiet moments after a battle. It had always been an enemy, a thief that stole what mattered most. But now, it felt different. Familiar. As if it wasn't a force acting against her but a companion walking beside her.

Emethy closed her eyes, exhaling slowly. She could still feel the cold presence of the shadow from that night, the way it had appeared out of nowhere and destroyed the creature sent by Alaric. It had moved with purpose, its power undeniable. But why her? Why spare her when it took others?

The questions gnawed at her, and for the first time, she found herself wanting answers. *If I could meet it, speak to it... maybe I could understand.* The thought lingered, dangerous and enticing. Yet she kept it to herself, unwilling to share it even with Lyra, let alone the others. They wouldn't understand.

Back at the camp, Kellan was stoking the fire, his usual mischievous grin plastered across his face as he exchanged glances with Ploma. Darion stood nearby, sharpening his blade with a focus that seemed too intense to be casual. Ploma noticed his glances toward the forest—or more accurately, toward where Emethy had disappeared.

"You know, you don't have to pretend to be indifferent," Ploma said, her voice teasing but kind. "It's obvious you care about her."

Darion didn't look up, his hands continuing their rhythmic motion over the blade. "She can take care of herself," he said simply.

"Oh, we know she can," Kellan chimed in, leaning back against a log. "But that doesn't mean you don't care. And frankly, you're terrible at hiding it."

Darion paused for a moment, his jaw tightening. "You two have a lot of opinions," he said dryly, his tone laced with subtle irritation.

"We're just saying," Ploma added, sharing a knowing look with Kellan. "She doesn't let people in easily. But with you, it's different. She's different."

Darion finally looked up, his piercing blue eyes narrowing slightly. "She's... complicated," he admitted reluctantly. Elara—strong yet fragile, distant yet caring. Complicated as hell."

Kellan laughed, clapping Darion on the shoulder. "That's Emethy for you. And you're hopelessly drawn to it, aren't you?"

Darion shrugged off Kellan's hand, his expression unreadable. "I'm here because of orders. That's all."

Ploma snorted. "Sure you are. And I'm a queen."

When Emethy finally returned to the camp, Darion glanced at her briefly before returning to his blade. Kellan and Ploma exchanged sly grins, which Emethy didn't miss.

"What?" she asked, narrowing her eyes.

"Oh, nothing," Kellan said innocently, leaning back with exaggerated ease. "Just wondering how long it'll take for you two to admit what's obvious to the rest of us."

Emethy frowned, glancing at Darion, who looked equally unimpressed. "What's obvious?" she asked cautiously.

"That you and our brooding soldier here have a thing," Ploma said with a smirk.

Emethy's face flushed. "There's no 'thing.' Don't be ridiculous." She crossed her arms, glaring at them. "Darion is... Darion. That's it."

Darion didn't even look up, though there was a faint twitch at the corner of his mouth. "I'm flattered by the enthusiasm," he said dryly, "but I think you're reading too much into things."

Kellan chuckled. "Sure, sure. Keep telling yourselves that."

Emethy huffed, grabbing a piece of bread and sitting down as far from Darion as possible. But the blush on her cheeks didn't go unnoticed.

As the night wore on and the fire crackled softly, Emethy's thoughts drifted back to the shadow. While the others laughed and teased each other, she stared into the flames, her mind spinning.

I have to know, she thought, her resolve hardening. I have to find a way to meet Death.

Chapter 29

The Return of the Lost

The forest was quiet as Emethy wandered through the dense trees, the soft crunch of leaves under her boots the only sound in the stillness. The air was thick with the scent of pine and earth, and faint streams of moonlight pierced through the canopy above, illuminating her path in silvery streaks. She wasn't sure why she had ventured so far from the workshop, but something in her heart pulled her forward—an unspoken desire to understand the shadow that loomed over her life.

Death, she thought, the word heavy in her mind. It had saved her more times than she could count, yet it remained an enigma. Why did it intervene? Why her? It wasn't supposed to protect; it was supposed to take.

She paused near a clearing, her gaze lifting to the stars scattered like diamonds across the sky. "Why do you follow me?" she murmured aloud, her voice barely above a whisper. "What do you want from me?"

The stillness around her deepened, and for a moment, she thought she might have imagined the faint shift in the air. But then she felt it—a chill that brushed against her skin like icy fingertips. The shadows around her seemed to thicken, coalescing into a form just beyond the edge of the clearing.

Emethy's breath hitched as the shadow took shape, its edges flickering like smoke caught in an unseen wind. The presence was unmistakable.

"You," she whispered, her voice trembling. "You're here."

The figure didn't speak, but its form shifted closer, the darkness around it pulsating with an otherworldly energy. Emethy felt rooted to the spot, her heart pounding in her chest. She wanted to run, but at the same time, she was drawn to it, her curiosity outweighing her fear.

"Why?" she asked again, louder this time. "Why do you save me? What am I to you?"

The shadow remained silent, but something stirred within her mind—a voice, faint and distant, like a whisper carried on the wind.

"You are not ready to know".

Emethy's brows furrowed, frustration bubbling to the surface. "Not ready? You've been following me, intervening in my life, and you won't even tell me why? That's not fair!"

The voice came again, softer this time, but tinged with an undeniable finality.

"Soon, you will understand".

Before she could respond, the shadow began to dissipate, its form unraveling like threads pulled from a tapestry. Emethy took a step forward, desperation clawing at her. "Wait!" she bawled out of frustration. "Don't go! Please, I need answers!"

But the shadow was gone, leaving only the cold stillness of the forest behind. Emethy stood there, her fists clenched at her sides, tears of frustration prickling her eyes. She felt the weight of the unanswered questions pressing down on her, suffocating in their enormity.

When Emethy returned to the camp, the fire had burned low, its embers glowing faintly in the darkness. Kellan was sprawled on a log, snoring softly, while Ploma was wrapped in a blanket nearby. Darion, however, was still awake, his sharp gaze immediately locking onto her as she approached.

"You've been gone a while," he said, his tone neutral but edged with concern.

Emethy shrugged, avoiding his eyes as she sat down near the fire. "I needed some air."

Darion didn't press further, but his eyes lingered on her for a moment longer before he returned to sharpening his blade. The rhythmic scrape of metal on stone filled the silence between them.

"Did you find what you were looking for?" he asked after a while, his voice quieter this time.

Emethy hesitated, her gaze fixed on the dying flames. "Not yet," she admitted. "But I will."

Darion nodded, his expression unreadable. "Good," he said simply. "Because whatever it is, we'll face it together."

Emethy glanced at him, surprised by the certainty in his voice. She opened her mouth to respond, but the words caught in her throat. Instead, she gave a small nod, her heart feeling just a little lighter despite the lingering shadows in her mind.

As the fire crackled softly, Emethy leaned back against the log, her thoughts still restless but her resolve stronger than ever. Whatever the shadow—Death—wanted, she would find out. And she wouldn't stop until she had the answers she sought.

The moon hung low in the sky, its pale glow casting an ethereal light over the dense forest. Though the pink moon was still three days away, its impending arrival seemed to charge the air with an almost imperceptible hum. Emethy moved carefully through the trees, her boots crunching softly against the dried leaves. The air was cool, carrying with it a strange stillness that made her uneasy. She didn't know what drew her out here tonight, but something about the moon's approach seemed to call to her, urging her forward.

Her thoughts swirled, filled with fragments of unanswered questions about Death and the connection it seemed to have with her. She wanted answers, and though she was unaware Alaric would be nearby, something about the forest tonight felt different—as if it were leading her to a confrontation she couldn't yet foresee.

As she stepped into a small clearing, a shadow moved at the edge of her vision. Emethy froze, her hand instinctively moving to the hilt of the small dagger at her belt. But before she could draw it, a voice broke the silence.

"I knew you'd come this far," Alaric's voice said, smooth and familiar, sending a chill down her spine.

She turned slowly, her eyes narrowing as she caught sight of him stepping out from behind a tree. He was dressed in dark, fitted clothing that blended with the shadows, his expression calm but predatory. His presence filled the clearing, radiating the quiet arrogance of someone who knew they held the upper hand.

"Alaric," she said, her voice steady despite the way her heart pounded in her chest. "I should have known it was you."

"Did you miss me?" he asked, his tone mocking as he took a step closer. "You've been running for so long, Emethy. It's exhausting, isn't it?"

Emethy's grip on her dagger tightened, but she didn't draw it. Instead, she took a slow breath, her mind racing. *If I go with him willingly, perhaps I'll have a chance to meet Death again. Perhaps it will answer my questions.*

"What do you want, Alaric?" she asked, keeping her tone neutral.

His eyes gleamed in the moonlight. "You know what I want. You. Back at the palace. Back where you belong."

She let out a bitter laugh. "I don't belong to anyone."

"That's where you're wrong," Alaric said, his smile sharp. "You belong to me, Emethy. You always have."

He lunged forward before she could respond, grabbing her wrist and twisting the dagger from her grip. Emethy didn't resist much, her decision made. She met his gaze with defiance but didn't struggle as he forced her hands behind her back.

"You're making this easier than I expected," Alaric remarked, his tone edged with curiosity. "What's your game, Emethy? Why aren't you fighting?"

"Maybe I'm tired of running," Emethy replied, her voice calm. "Maybe I'm curious to see what you think you can accomplish."

Alaric frowned, his grip tightening slightly. "You're hiding something. But no matter. You'll talk when the time comes."

He began leading her deeper into the forest, his pace quick and deliberate. Emethy followed without protest, her mind racing. *If Death is watching, it will come. It has to.*

Back at the camp, Darion was pacing near the fire, his sharp eyes scanning the darkened edges of the clearing.

Ploma watched him with growing concern, her hands wringing nervously.

"She said she went out for a walk," Ploma said, her voice uncertain. "But that was hours ago. She usually doesn't stay out this long."

Darion stopped pacing, his jaw tightening. "And you didn't think to tell me sooner?" he snapped, the frustration in his voice barely restrained.

Ploma flinched slightly but held her ground. "I thought she needed time. You know how she gets when she's thinking about something."

Darion ran a hand through his hair, exhaling sharply. "It's getting dark. She shouldn't be out there alone."

Kellan, who had been sitting quietly, stood and placed a hand on Darion's shoulder. "We'll find her," he said firmly. "Let's split up and search the area. She couldn't have gone far."

Darion shook his head. "I'll look for her. Alone." He grabbed his sword and turned toward the trees, his expression set with grim determination.

"Darion," Ploma began, but he didn't stop. "Be careful," she called after him, her voice laced with worry.

As Darion moved swiftly through the forest, his senses were on high alert. The faint light of the moon guided his steps, but the shadows seemed to stretch endlessly in every direction. He replayed Emethy's recent behavior in his mind—the way she had been distant, lost in thought. She had been hiding something, he was sure of it.

What if Alaric took her? The thought sent a surge of anger through him, his grip tightening on his sword. *Or worse... what if Death came for her?*

The idea unsettled him more than he wanted to admit. He had seen the shadow before, felt its cold presence. It was a force beyond his understanding, and the thought of it taking Emethy filled him with a sense of helplessness he despised—a helplessness he had felt once before when he couldn't save his sister. He refused to let that happen again. Not to her.

As he pressed deeper into the forest, he caught sight of faint tracks in the dirt. Two sets of footprints, one lighter and hesitant, the other heavier and deliberate. His heart sank. *Alaric.*

Darion quickened his pace, his resolve hardening. Whatever Alaric's plans were, he wouldn't let them succeed. And if Death had its own agenda, then it would have to contend with him first.

Chapter 30

The Gathering Storm

The grand halls of Alaric's palace loomed dark and oppressive, lit only by sparse torches that cast flickering shadows on the stone walls. Emethy's footsteps echoed in the vast corridor as Alaric dragged her by the arm, his grip firm and unyielding. Her heart raced, not from fear of Alaric, but from the unexpected sight that had stopped her cold moments earlier—Lyra. The spirit hovered silently, her small figure faintly glowing, her eyes wide with urgency.

Lyra? Emethystin had thought as she caught the girl's familiar form flitting through the shadows. But Lyra had given no time for questions, whispering as she hovered beside Emethy.

"Emethy, listen to me," Lyra said in her soft, hurried voice. "He has your aunt Marella. She's in one of the chambers… trapped. I followed her here."

Emethy's stomach twisted, dread pooling in her chest. *Aunt Marella? Here?* She barely had time to process Lyra's words before Alaric's rough tug pulled her forward again, the spirit falling behind. Lyra's glow dimmed as they neared a large set of double doors at the end of the hallway. She hovered just outside, stopping in her tracks.

"I can't go in," Lyra said, her voice tinged with frustration. "The Crooked King can see me. Be careful, Emethy."

Before Emethy could respond, Alaric yanked the doors open and dragged her inside.

The room was vast and dimly lit, the air heavy with the scent of old parchment and decay. At the center of the room, seated in an ornate but tarnished grand chair with wheels, was the Crooked King. His form was hunched, his frail body covered in layers of dark, regal robes. His eyes, though sunken and shadowed, burned with a sharp, malevolent light that seemed to pierce through the soul.

Alaric threw Emethy forward, and she stumbled, catching herself before she fell. She straightened, meeting the king's gaze with defiance despite the unease curling in her stomach.

"Father," Alaric said, his voice smooth and confident, "I have her. The girl who will reverse your curse."

The Crooked King tilted his head, his skeletal hand gripping the armrest of his chair. His voice, when it came, was dry and rasping, like wind through brittle leaves. "This is her?" he asked, his gaze sweeping over Emethy with a mix of disdain and curiosity.

Alaric nodded. "Yes. She has the mark, the abilities… everything we need. By the time of the pink moon, your curse will be lifted, and you'll walk again as you once did."

Emethy's eyes narrowed. *The mark? My abilities?* Her birthmark burned faintly beneath her clothing as if in response, and she clenched her fists, anger flaring in her chest. "I'm not here to help you," she said coldly, her voice steady despite the tremor of fear beneath it.

The Crooked King let out a dry chuckle, his thin lips curling into a sinister smile. "It matters not what you're here for, child. Your defiance is meaningless. You will serve your purpose, whether you wish to or not."

Alaric smirked, standing tall beside his father. "You've run long enough, Emethystin. This is where it ends."

Emethy's mind raced, her thoughts jumping between Lyra's warning about Marella, the king's cryptic words, and the burning anger that coursed through her. But one thought stood out above the rest: she needed to survive, to find her aunt, and to stop whatever dark plan Alaric and his father had for her.

Outside the chamber, Lyra hovered near the closed doors, her small form flickering with agitation. She could hear fragments of the conversation within, her ghostly fingers curling into fists. She wanted to rush in, to help Emethy, but the Crooked King's ability to see spirits kept her at bay.

Emethy, stay strong, she thought, her glow dimming slightly as she drifted back into the shadows to avoid being seen by the passing guards. *I'll find a way to help you... I promise.*

The stone walls of the palace loomed ominously as Darion crept along the shadowed perimeter. The night was silent, save for the faint rustling of leaves and the occasional clink of armor from the guards patrolling below. He had tracked Emethy to this place, his heart pounding with the urgency of finding her. Losing her wasn't an option—not after everything he had already lost.

Scaling the outer wall, Darion moved with practiced precision, his fingers gripping the cold stone as he ascended. His breath was steady, his movements deliberate. Each foothold brought him closer to the window he had seen faintly lit from a distance. *"She has to be in there"*, he thought, his resolve hardening.

When he reached the ledge, he peered inside. The chamber was dimly lit by a single candle. And there she was—Emethy, sitting on the edge of a grand but cold bed, her head bowed, her expression distant. Relief flooded through Darion as he pushed the window open and slipped inside silently.

As he stepped into the room, Emethy looked up sharply, her breath catching. "Darion? What are you doing here?" she asked, her voice a mix of disbelief and worry.

Darion's jaw tightened as he moved closer. "This isn't who you are," he said, his tone low but firm, his piercing blue eyes locking onto hers. "You're not someone who gives up."

Emethy's lips trembled, and she stood, her fists clenching at her sides. "And this isn't who you are," she shot back, her voice soft but filled with emotion. "You don't take risks like this."

Emethy startled at the sound of soft footsteps. When she looked up and saw Darion standing there, her eyes widened in disbelief. "Darion?" she whispered, her voice barely audible. his voice barely above a breath. "Emeth…"

He moved toward her quickly, his piercing blue eyes scanning her as if to ensure she was unharmed. "I told you I'd find you," he said, his voice low but steady.

"You shouldn't be here," she said, her tone laced with worry and anger. "It's dangerous. If they find you—"

"I don't care," Darion interrupted, stepping closer. "I couldn't let them keep you here. I couldn't lose you."

Her lips trembled, and before she could say another word, he pulled her into his arms. The embrace was firm, desperate, and filled with unspoken emotion. For a moment, the world outside the chamber ceased to exist.

"You're an idiot," she murmured against his chest, her voice breaking slightly.

"Probably," he replied, a faint smirk tugging at his lips. "But I'm your idiot."

Emethy tilted her head up to look at him, her heart pounding as their eyes locked. In his eyes, she saw a storm of emotions—worry, resolve, and something deeper that he could no longer hide. In that moment, the world around them faded. She let herself forget the danger and the darkness, surrendering to the fragile connection they had built. Slowly, she leaned in, her lips brushing his in a tentative gesture. The kiss deepened, an unspoken promise passing between them—a shared understanding of the risks, the sacrifices, and the feelings they could no longer deny.

The door to the chamber burst open with a loud crash, and Prince Alaric stormed in, his expression a mix of fury and disbelief. "Well, isn't this a cozy scene?" he sneered, his voice dripping with venom.

Emethy and Darion broke apart, their shock mirrored in each other's eyes. Darion moved in front of Emethy protectively, his body shielding her from Alaric's gaze.

Alaric's eyes burned with jealousy as he stepped closer, pointing an accusatory finger at Emethy. "So this is why you ran?" he spat, his voice laced with venom. "You couldn't wait to throw yourself into someone else's arms? After everything I did for you, Emethy, this is how you repay me? By betraying me?"

Emethy flinched at his words, her fists clenching at her sides. "You never did anything for me," she said coldly, her voice trembling with restrained anger. "You only ever wanted to use me."

Before Alaric could respond, Darion stepped forward, his voice low and dangerous. "Watch your tongue," he said, his eyes narrowing. "You don't get to talk to her like that."

Alaric's gaze snapped to Darion, and his lips curled into a cruel smile. "And you," he said, his voice mocking. "My loyal soldier, reduced to this? Falling for her lies, betraying me for her? How pathetic."

"I follow my own path now," Darion said firmly, his stance unwavering. "And I'll protect her from you, no matter the cost."

Alaric's face darkened with rage, and he stepped back, clapping his hands. Guards flooded into the room, their weapons drawn. "Take him," Alaric ordered, his voice cold and commanding.

Darion fought valiantly, his sword flashing as he held off the guards. Emethy watched in horror, her body frozen by Alaric's earlier spell, unable to move to help him.

"Darion!" she cried, her voice breaking as he was overwhelmed by the sheer number of guards.

The last thing she saw before darkness clouded her vision was Darion being dragged away, blood staining his armor, his head held high even in defeat. As Alaric loomed over her, his cruel smile returned. "After the ritual, you'll sleep in my bed," he said, his voice dripping with possessiveness. "You are mine, Emethy. Only mine."

When Emethy regained awareness, she was alone in the chamber, her body heavy with the lingering effects of the spell. Regret clawed at her heart, sharp and unrelenting. *What have I done?* she thought, tears streaming down her face. She had allowed herself to be taken, believing she could manipulate the situation, but now Darion was paying the price. As she whispered his name, the weight of her choices crushed her, leaving her feeling more helpless than ever. "Darion..."

In the hall outside, Lyra hovered near the shadows, her small form flickering with frustration and fear. *I have to help her,* she thought. *I can't let this happen.*

The spirit turned and darted down the hallway, her mind racing as she formulated a plan to free Darion and save Emethy from Alaric's clutches.

Inside the chamber, Emethy whispered, "Lyra... are you there?"

The small spirit materialized softly, her glow dim as she floated closer. "I'm here," Lyra said, her voice filled with worry. "Emethy, what's wrong? You're crying."

Emethy shook her head, her voice trembling. "This is my fault, Lyra. I thought I could control this. I thought I could outsmart Alaric. But now... Darion is suffering because of me."

Lyra hovered beside her, her expression pained. "He fought for you. I've never seen him fight like that before. He cares about you, Emethy."

Emethy looked away, tears streaming down her face. "He doesn't even know how to care for someone properly, yet he tries. He's stubborn, avoidant... but he's been there for me in ways no one else has. And I... I let him down."

Lyra's small voice softened. "You can't change what's already happened. But you can still save him. Darion believes in you, Emethy. You have to believe in yourself too."

Emethy wiped her tears, her jaw tightening as resolve began to harden in her chest. "You're right," she said, her voice steadier now. "I'll get him out of this, no matter what it takes. I owe him that."

Lyra gave a small, encouraging nod. "We'll figure it out together. You're not alone in this."

Chapter 31

The Final Hunt of the Pink Moon

The grand hall of the palace was suffused with an eerie light as the pink moon hung high in the sky, casting its glow through the stained-glass windows. The air was heavy with tension, each breath thick with anticipation and dread. Torches lined the walls, their flames flickering uneasily as if aware of the dark purpose the night held.

Emethy was brought into the hall, her hands bound loosely in front of her, though the weight of her chains was nothing compared to the turmoil in her heart. Her birthmark burned beneath her clothing, a searing heat that was both painful and unnervingly alive. She raised her head, her eyes scanning the room, and there, at the center of it all, sat the Crooked King.

The king's skeletal frame slouched in his grand chair with wheels, his sunken eyes gleaming with malevolent delight. Alaric stood beside him, his regal posture betraying his smug satisfaction. Behind them, a raised dais held a stone altar inscribed with ancient runes, glowing faintly under the moonlight.

As Emethy's gaze swept across the room, it landed on Darion. He was in chains, kneeling near the corner, his face battered but his eyes burning with defiance. Her heart twisted at the sight of him, but she forced herself to stay composed.

"Ah, the guest of honor," the king rasped, his voice dry and grating. "Welcome, child. You will soon fulfill the destiny that has been prepared for you."

Emethy's jaw tightened, but she said nothing. Her mind raced, searching for a way out, for a plan, for anything.

Alaric stepped forward, a triumphant smile playing on his lips. "You've been defiant for far too long, Emethy," he said, his tone smooth but cold. "But tonight, that ends."

He clapped his hands, and the heavy doors at the far end of the hall creaked open. Two guards entered, dragging someone between them. Emethy's breath caught as

Aunt Marella was brought forward, her face pale but resolute.

"Marella," Emethy whispered, her voice trembling.

"Emethy, don't—" Marella began, but Alaric cut her off with a sharp gesture.

"Spare us the dramatics," Alaric said, his voice dripping with contempt. He turned to Emethy, his expression darkening. "You will perform the ritual. You will do as you are told. Or she dies."

Emethy's hands clenched into fists, her nails biting into her palms. The searing heat of her birthmark intensified, almost as if it were alive, reacting to her fury and desperation. She glanced at Marella, then at Darion, whose gaze met hers, steady and unwavering.

Two guards forced Emethy toward the stone altar, where Alaric motioned for her to stand. Her legs felt heavy, as though the weight of the moment threatened to crush her. The glowing runes on the altar pulsed rhythmically, matching the rapid beat of her heart.

"Do it," Alaric commanded, his voice sharp.

Emethy hesitated, her mind racing. The king's skeletal smile widened. "You hesitate, child. Do you think you have a choice?"

Alaric gestured to Marella, and one of the guards drew a blade, holding it to her throat. "Now, Emethy," he growled. "Or her blood will spill."

Tears burned in Emethy's eyes as she looked at Marella, who shook her head slightly. "Don't do it, Emethy," she said softly. "Don't give them what they want."

Emethy's birthmark flared suddenly, its glow spilling through the fabric of her clothing, casting the room in an ethereal light. Gasps echoed through the hall as the mark's radiance grew, pulsing with a power that seemed to resonate with the pink moon above.

Darion struggled against his chains, his voice cutting through the tension. "Emethy, don't listen to them! You don't owe them anything!"

Alaric turned sharply, his face twisting with anger. "Silence him!" he barked. A guard stepped forward, striking Darion across the face, but the soldier's defiant glare never wavered.

"You think this will break her?" Darion spat, blood trickling from the corner of his mouth. "You don't know her at all."

Darion reached the clearing, his breaths ragged, his body barely able to carry him forward. The brutal torture he endured had left him weakened, his legs threatening to give out beneath him. His armor was streaked with blood, his vision blurred from exhaustion, but none of it mattered when he saw Emethy bound at the altar. A surge of fury and desperation pushed him forward, his voice raw as he called out, "Emethy!"

Emethy's head snapped toward him, her eyes widening in shock and relief. "Darion!"

Before he could take another step, Alaric's soldiers swarmed him. Darion fought valiantly, his sword cutting through the air with relentless precision. But the sheer number of guards overwhelmed him. A blow to his side sent him stumbling, and another strike to his leg brought him to his knees.

"Emethy..." he whispered, his vision blurring as blood dripped from a wound on his temple.

The guards seized him, forcing him to his feet. Darion struggled weakly, his body battered and broken, but his eyes never left Emethy.

Back at the altar, Alaric began to chant, his voice resonating with an otherworldly power. The air grew thick with energy, the symbols on the altar glowing brighter as the ritual progressed. Emethy struggled against her bindings, her heart pounding as she felt the unnatural pull of the ritual.

"Alaric, stop this!" she shouted, her voice breaking. "You don't know what will happen!"

Alaric's smile widened, his hands raised to the heavens. "That's where you're wrong, Emethy. I know exactly what will happen. The Pink Moon's power will awaken the true potential within you—and bind it to me."

Her blood ran cold at his words. She pulled harder against the chains, her birthmark glowing faintly as her desperation grew.

Emethy's heart shattered as she watched Darion dragged toward the altar, his body limp and bloodied. "Let him go!" she screamed, her voice echoing into the night.

Alaric chuckled darkly. "He's a fool to think he could challenge me. But don't worry, Emethy. He'll witness the moment you and I reshape destiny."

As Darion was thrown to the ground near the altar, Emethy ran to him, her chains clinking with each step. She knelt beside him, tears streaming down her face as she placed her hands on his bloodied armor. "Darion, stay with me," she whispered, her voice trembling. "Please, don't leave me."

Darion's eyes fluttered open, and he managed a weak smile. "I'm not going anywhere," he rasped. "I came for you... I'll always come for you."

Emethy's birthmark began to glow brighter, responding to her overwhelming emotions. The guards stepped back, unease flickering across their faces. Alaric, however, stood unfazed, his focus still on the ritual.

Summoning all her remaining strength, Emethy seized a fallen sword, its hilt cold in her trembling hands. She turned to Alaric, her gaze burning with defiance. With a smirk, Alaric drew his own blade, their weapons clashing in a burst of sparks.

Emethy's muscles screamed in protest as she fought, her movements sluggish under the weight of Alaric's spell. Her vision blurred, her energy draining rapidly. Alaric pressed forward, his strikes precise and relentless. She stumbled but held firm, determination fueling her as their swords clashed again and again. Alaric was able to knock her down.

Emethy's breath came in short, sharp gasps as the light from her birthmark grew blinding, the heat coursing through her veins like wildfire. The runes on the altar responded, their glow intensifying until they matched the mark's brilliance. The king leaned forward in his chair, his eyes wide with greed.

"Yes," he whispered. "The power is awakening. Continue, child. Fulfill your destiny."

But Emethy's gaze wasn't on the king. It wasn't on Alaric or the altar. It was on Darion and Marella. Her voice was steady when she spoke, though it carried the weight of her anguish. "You want my power? Fine." Her words faltered as Alaric stepped closer, taking her hand roughly. With a swift motion, he drew a blade across her palm. Blood welled up, dripping onto the glowing runes of the altar, which flared with sudden intensity. Emethy winced, her voice trembling but resolute. "But you don't get to control me."

The glow from her birthmark flared once more, and with it, the torches around the hall extinguished, plunging the room into darkness save for the blinding light emanating from her. The runes on the altar pulsed violently, and suddenly, a shadow emerged from the light—an ominous, towering presence. The room fell deathly silent as a deep, resonant voice echoed through the chamber.

"Who dares to spill my blood?" the shadow growled, its form coalescing into a figure cloaked in pure darkness. Its piercing, glowing eyes locked onto the Crooked King, who froze in his chair, his frail body trembling with fear.

"Death," Emethy whispered, her voice trembling with awe and fear. The shadow turned its gaze to her for a brief moment, and she felt an overwhelming connection, as if it recognized her as its own.

"You dare to claim what is mine?" the shadow roared, its voice filled with fury that shook the very walls. Blue flames erupted from its form, engulfing the Crooked

King. His screams echoed briefly before his body was reduced to scattering across the floor.

Alaric stood paralyzed, his face pale and his confidence shattered. "What... what is this?" he stammered, his voice weak as he stumbled backward.

The shadow turned its attention to Alaric, its presence suffocating. "You seek to defile her power," it said in a low, threatening tone. "You do not understand what you have awakened."

Emethy watched in stunned silence, her heart pounding. She glanced at Aunt Marella, who stood remarkably calm, her expression unreadable.

"I knew it," Marella murmured softly, her eyes fixed on the shadow. "You were never just anyone, Emethy. You've always belonged to her."

The shadow loomed over Alaric but didn't strike. Before it could dissipate, the Crooked King, trembling in his chair, rasped out with a twisted smile, "Every time Death comes, it takes someone away. This time, it has to be me, my son." His voice cracked, his skeletal hand reaching weakly toward Alaric.

The shadow paused, its glowing eyes narrowing as it turned back to the king. Flames erupted from its form, engulfing the Crooked King completely, silencing his final words with a brief, agonized scream. Ashes scattered to the ground, and the shadow turned its attention back to Alaric, its presence suffocating.

As the chaos unfolded, Emethy felt something stir deep within her—a force far greater than she could comprehend. She didn't know if it was the pink moon, the birthmark, or something else entirely. But one thing was certain: this was only the beginning.

Chapter 32

When Death Called Her Name

The grand hall was silent, the air heavy with ash and the lingering scent of fire. The Crooked King was no more, his body reduced to nothing, but dust scattered across the floor. All eyes were on the towering shadow that loomed in the center of the room. Its presence was suffocating, its power undeniable. The shadow, Death itself, turned its piercing, glowing eyes toward Emethy, and for the first time, she felt truly seen.

"Who has dared to challenge my domain and spill the blood that binds us?" Death's voice reverberated through the hall, low and resonant, shaking the very foundation of the palace. The question hung in the air, a challenge to all who stood before it.

Alaric stumbled backward, his face pale and his confidence shattered. He couldn't speak, couldn't move, as the shadow's gaze briefly flicked to him before returning to Emethy.

"You," Death said, addressing Emethy directly. Its tone softened, yet remained commanding. "You are not merely a mortal. You are my blood, my legacy."

Emethy's breath caught in her throat. "What are you saying?" she whispered, her voice trembling.

The shadow loomed closer, the room growing colder with its presence. "You are my daughter," it declared. "Born to walk the path between life and afterlife. That mark on your shoulder is no mere birthmark; it is a sigil of your destiny."

The weight of the revelation hit Emethy like a tidal wave. Her mind raced with memories—moments of seeing spirits, of hearing whispers from the beyond, of feeling a pull toward the unknown. It all began to make sense.

"That is why I have always protected you," Death continued. "You are meant to bring balance, to guide lost souls to liberation. The spirits you see, the voices you hear—they are drawn to you because you are the bridge between worlds."

Emethy's knees buckled, and she would have fallen if not for Darion, who had struggled to his feet despite his chains. He caught her, his strong arms steadying her as she looked up at Death, her face pale but determined.

"I don't understand," Emethy said, her voice breaking. "Why me? Why this?"

"Because it is who you are," Death replied simply. "Your purpose is greater than you can comprehend. The world of the living and the realm of the dead are imbalanced. You will be the one to restore harmony."

As Death spoke, the room began to shift. The shadows seemed to expand, and suddenly, figures began to appear. Translucent forms emerged from the darkness, their eyes fixed on Emethy. They were spirits, countless souls lingering between worlds, their presence filling the hall.

Emethy's breath hitched as she recognized one among them. "Lyra," she whispered. The small spirit floated toward her, her eyes filled with a mixture of sorrow and relief.

"Emethy," Lyra said softly, her gaze shifting toward Death. "It reminds me of Malentha... the same aura, the same cold certainty. Was it you who took her?"

Death's glowing eyes flicked toward Lyra, its presence still and commanding. "I did not take her," it said slowly, its voice reverberating like a distant storm. "She is me. Malentha and I are one and the same. She walked her path as mortal, and now, she fulfills her purpose as Death. It was always meant to be."

Tears welled in Emethy's eyes as she looked around, seeing more and more spirits gathering. They were watching her, waiting for her. She felt their pain, their longing, and their hope.

"They're all here because of you," Death said. "They require you. You will guide them to the peace they seek. This is your calling."

In the midst of the chaos, Emethy's gaze shifted to Aunt Marella. Unlike the others, Marella's face was calm, her eyes betraying no surprise.

"You knew," Emethy said, her voice shaking. "You knew all along."

Marella stepped forward, her expression softening. "I suspected," she admitted. "Your mother... she told me you were special. That you were meant for something greater. But I didn't know it would be this."

Emethy's hands trembled. "Why didn't you tell me?"

"Because it wasn't my truth to tell," "YOU BELONG TO DEATH" Marella said gently. "You had to discover it on your own, in your own time."

Death began to dissipate, its form unraveling into tendrils of shadow that lingered in the air. But before it faded completely, it turned to Emethy one last time. Death said *"You have known me longer than most."*

Elara replied *without looking, voice calm but firm "I do not fear you."*

Death *a soft sigh, neither sorrowful nor amused "Yet you never welcome me."*

Elara *her fingers tighten around her dagger, knuckles pale "Why should I? You take without mercy. You steal without reason."*

Death *pauses, then speaks as if reciting a truth as old as time "I do only what must be done. It is not cruelty, nor kindness. It simply is."*

Elara *her breath sharpens, bitterness laced in her words* "That does not make it any less cruel."

Death *watching her, voice unreadable* "Hate me if you must. It changes nothing. All roads, in the end, lead to me."

Elara *turns to face the darkness where Death lingers, her gaze unwavering* "Then I will walk slowly."

Death *a moment of silence, then a whisper like a fading wind* "As you wish, little flame."

"You have the strength within you," it said. "Do not fear your purpose. Embrace it. You are not alone. I will always be watching."

Emethystin stood in the center of the hall, surrounded by spirits, her heart heavy but resolute. She turned to Darion, who still stood by her side, his gaze steady and unwavering.

"What now?" he asked softly.

Emethystin took a deep breath, her birthmark still faintly glowing. She glanced toward Death, her expression clouded with a mix of defiance and sorrow. "I don't understand," she said, her voice trembling. "You've taken so much from me. How am I supposed to trust you? To believe in a purpose that caused me so much pain?"

Death turned its glowing eyes toward her, its form cold and unyielding. "Trust is irrelevant," it said, its voice devoid of emotion. "What must be done will be done, regardless of what you think or feel. I am not here for understanding. I am here to fulfill what is necessary."

Emethy's hands trembled, her fists clenching at her sides. "You don't care," she said bitterly. "You don't care about anyone."

Death loomed closer, its presence as oppressive as ever. "Care is a mortal weakness," it said, its tone neither defensive nor apologetic. "You will know, in time, that there is no purpose in questioning inevitability."

Lyra hovered closer to Emethy, her voice gentle but uncertain. "Emethy... maybe it's not about caring. Maybe it's about balance. That's what Malentha would have said."

Death's form began to dissipate, its voice echoing faintly as it faded. "You will understand soon," it said, leaving the hall in a cold, heavy silence.

And with that, the shadow disappeared, leaving the hall in silence.

As the spirits around her began to fade, guided by her newfound power, Emethy knew Her path was still unfolding, with many challenges and discoveries ahead. But for the first time, she felt ready to face it. The daughter of Death had found her path...

"Only those who have walked through darkness understand the weight of the light."

Dear Reader,

Thank you for stepping into the world of *"Emethystin"*. This story is more than just a tale of magic, darkness, and destiny—it's a journey of resilience, self-discovery, and the choices that shape us. Elara's path is not an easy one, but neither is life. Through loss, mystery, and the whispers of the unseen, she dares to walk forward, and I hope her story resonates with the fire within you.

To those who have ever felt lost, out of place, or burdened by the past—you are not alone. May Emeth's strength inspire yours, and may you find solace in the echoes of her journey. Only readers with highly intelligence of emotions can grasp this novel.

Thank you for being a part of this adventure. Your support means the world.

With gratitude,
Maya :)

www.ingramcontent.com/pod-product-compliance
Lightning Source LLC
LaVergne TN
LVHW091701070526
838199LV00050B/2232